Drawn Away

Millie Curtis

Avid Readers Publishing Group
Lakewood, California

Drawn Away

Avid Readers Publishing Group

http://www.avidreaderspg.com

ISBN-13: 978-1-61286-374-0

Acknowledgements

Many thanks to Amy Nishimoto for her hours of editing and to Elizabeth Blye for her assistance with photography and cover design. Also to those who are preserving history by renovating Stone's Chapel in Clarke County, which gave me the inspiration to write this novel.

Chapter 1

This Sunday morning started out like every Sunday morning. Father and two of my brothers were out doing farm chores, my older sister was helping in the kitchen where Mother was hurrying about as she always did. Breakfast needed to be on the table and over before we went to church.

I was getting my younger sister and brother ready for the ten o'clock service at Stone's Chapel. "You two better stay clean before we have to leave." Those were wasted words. What do four and five-year-olds know about staying clean. I reasoned that scrambled eggs and scrapple were not mess makers and as long as there wasn't oatmeal to contend with, I was relatively safe if I put aprons over their Sunday go-to-meeting clothes. I knew I would be the one to clean them up again. I'm not sure why that designated duty fell to me, but it did.

My sister always helped with housework. Perhaps that was to get her ready for marriage. She had a steady beau, and it was an unspoken promise they would marry when he was able to buy his own farm. Of course, it was going on four years and he didn't show any signs of leaving his parents' place, which wasn't that prosperous. My sister still held hope. At twenty-two she wasn't getting any younger.

1

I didn't care much for her boyfriend Harold. He didn't show much ambition to my way of thinking, although he managed to look the part of a desirable catch.

Nora, my sister, was no raving beauty, but she was far from homely and there was beauty in her manner.

She was well-liked by young and old alike. Nora was a plain country girl. I thought she deserved better than a plodding man who kept her on a string for four years. What if that string broke? And, who was I to criticize? At eighteen going on nineteen, I had no prospects; not that I was actively looking for any.

On the occasions we went into the town of Berryville to get supplies, I would buy a McCall's magazine and dream about living in a big city like New York and wearing the lovely clothes worn by fashionable women. New York City was a far cry from living on a farm in rural Virginia. In the 1920's, the country was changing and I wanted to be a part of that.

One day when I was going through a magazine, my mother came into the room. "Don't waste your time and money dreaming about what can't be," Mother said. "You need to get serious about settling down just like your sister."

"I don't see a ring on her finger," I replied and regretted the words as soon as they flew out of my mouth.

"Vallie May. Don't be sassy, young lady!"

I remember saying I was sorry but I only half-meant it. Most of all because I detested the name, Vallie May. I had asked my mother where she came up with that awful name. She said it was for two things she loved; the Shenandoah Valley, where we lived, and the month of May, which brought beautiful flowers. "You were a ray of sunshine when you were born on that rainy day, so you were blessed with a beautiful name." Mother and I didn't always agree on what was beautiful. At least she had been somewhat creative by spelling my first name Vallie instead of Valley. I got kidded enough as it was.

Mother called from the kitchen. "Vallie, bring the children out and get them started before your father and brothers come in from the barn. Then you help me so Nora can get dressed before Harold comes to pick her up."

"We'll be right there," I answered. I turned to the two younger ones, who still looked half asleep, "It's time to eat. Don't spill anything on your clothes," I warned them as I rolled up the sleeves of Davey's shirt.

"You always say that," said Lucy. She looked up at me. "Why don't you have a boyfriend like Nora has?"

"Because I don't want a boyfriend like Nora has."

"Mother says Harold is a good steady man," Lucy replied.

I was tying her apron straps. "Your five-year-old ears pick up too much," I said to her. "Hurry out and take your places at the table before Father and the boys come in."

3

I followed them into the kitchen, took the children's plates Mother had prepared and set them on the table, pulled their chairs up close, and poured two small glasses of milk. "Don't spill the milk," I warned.

"You're mean, Vallie," said Davey.

"Please don't spill the milk," I said and smiled at my little brother. "Is that better?" Maybe I did sound mean, but I felt irritable for no reason that I knew. Perhaps it was the fact that we would have to sit like statues in the uncomfortable pews at church and pretend to listen to the windy Presbyterian minister. Every Sunday was the same. This was the first assignment for Wendell Stephens, six months out of divinity school, and I think he wanted to make a good impression. He would impress me and the younger set with a shorter sermon.

Father and the boys came into the big kitchen after they left their boots on the back porch. They still smelled like the barn and I lost my appetite, so I took a piece of bread and butter and went to dress for church.

I shared a room with Nora at the top of the stairs. We had a window where I looked out to check the weather. It was a nice June day, but I could see rain clouds in the distance. Nora was almost ready. "Do you think it's going to rain?" I asked her.

"Father says it may rain later this afternoon." She was pinning on her hat. "Harold will most likely bring the covered buggy, so it won't matter to me."

I had to ask, "Do you ever get tired of Harold? He doesn't have much ambition."

Nora ignored my question and checked her image in the mirror. "Vallie, your problem is that you expect too much from life. One of these days Harold will give me an engagement ring, but he wants to be financially set first."

"Seems to me if a man really wanted to get married, he wouldn't wait around for five years and let someone else grab his girl."

Nora gave me a sour look with her hand on the doorknob, "You read too many magazines. I don't see any man wanting my attention."

"Open your eyes. I see Billy Wood giving you the glances at church."

"You're supposed to be paying attention to the service not gawking around at the congregation." Nora was getting miffed.

"I don't gawk, and I get enough of Windy Wendell. He could say the meat of the sermon all in two minutes, not drag it out." Yes, I knew I was edgy that morning.

Nora opened the door. "You're a dreamer, Vallie May."

She knew using both my names would rankle me. I threw a pillow in her direction as the door closed.

Maybe I did have my head in the clouds, but I was helping Miss Adelaide over at the Lockwood estate until her baby arrived. She told me about how she had gone to Katherine Gibbs business school and had lived and worked in Washington, D.C. during the war. It all sounded exciting. Best of all was when Miss Fannie and Miss Lottie came to the big house and they all talked and laughed about times they spent in Colorado and California. I was busy cleaning around the house, but I could hear their conversations. Now Miss Fannie and Miss Addie were both in the family way and settled into the domestic role of life. I wondered if I would ever be fortunate enough to have such good memories.

Chapter 2

It was cooler inside the chapel than out-doors causing me to wish I had worn my shawl. Father seated us in the pew as he did every Sunday morning. Harold and Nora were already there when we arrived. I sat next to Nora, then Lucy and David, Mother, my teen-aged brothers, Luke and Mark. With all the Browns settled, Father took his place at the end next to the isle. We were squeezed together shoulder to shoulder, so I quickly warmed up. It would be more comfortable if Harold sat in the pew in front of us, but my parents said we should sit together as a family. Of course, Harold wasn't part of the family and I hoped he never would be. I don't know why Harold struck a discordant chord with me, but I think the feeling was mutual.

Speaking of chords, the organist leaned on the keys of the organ and we rose for the processional. The hymns were my favorite part of the service. The choir of about a dozen men and women led the procession with Windy Wendell following. They took their seats in front of the organist and Reverend Stephens mounted the altar.

I was glad to see that it was our usual organist as the substitute played every hymn as a dirge. We sang *Holy, Holy, Holy*, raising our voices to the rafters. Either people enjoyed singing or it was a way of release before the hour long service commenced.

We were in the middle of the church so the only people I could see were those in front of me. However, I was good at keeping my head straight and turning my eye, so I could see right and left. Billy Wood was in his usual spot in the next row to the right. Every time he replaced the hymnal, he would casually glance back at Nora. I must have planted a curious seed because I noticed Nora sneaking a peak in Billy's direction a few times.

I liked Billy. Close to thirty he was still a bachelor and worked hard at keeping his dairy farm going. He was a serious farmer and learned all he could about raising heavy milk producing cows.

I knew Harold raised game chickens, and I heard that he bet and won a lot of money at game fights. Nora didn't believe that tidbit of gossip, but I told her it just made sense. Otherwise, why would he raise that type of chicken? They were tough meat to eat and their eggs weren't like our hens. I guess Nora didn't want to believe Harold was a gambler.

There was noticeable restless movement toward the end of the sermon, but we made it through the service without too many stretches, wiggles, and yawns. I felt antsy myself.

When it was over I could hardly wait to get out of the chapel and into the fresh air. Today was a church picnic. Mother and Nora had packed up our food and utensils and would help with serving, while Father and the boys gave a hand at setting up tables and chairs. That left me to spread out a blanket and keep an eye on Lucy and Davey.

I found a nice spot for us on flat ground shaded by an oak tree. Lucy and Davey began playing tag. I thought it was good for them to get rid of their energy until I saw them chasing each other where the women had set up a drink table. Fast as I could run, I caught them both just as they were about to collide with the table. The momentum sent me off balance and the three of us tumbled to the ground. I looked up into the startled and disapproving eyes of two women who were to serve the drinks. With a beet red face of embarrassment, I picked myself up quickly and said, "Excuse me," before I hauled my younger siblings off and hurriedly ushered them to the other side of the chapel. There was a small pond and no person in sight. Some horses were hitched to conveyances waiting for their owners.

"You hurt my arm, Vallie," said Davey. "We weren't doing anything."

"If Mother or Father has seen that near disaster more than your arm will hurt. You have to pay attention." I had composed myself to a reasonable state. "You can throw some rocks in the pond if you want to." That was all they needed to hear and they raced to find stones. The cares of the past few minutes were forgotten.

"You're quick on your feet," came a pleasant voice behind me.

I reeled around and came face to face with a young man dressed in a tan linen sack suit, white shirt, bow tie and bowler straw hat. He wasn't dressed like our local boys.

"I'm Ashton Corbin," he introduced himself. "I had to smile when I saw the near collision. That would have been a sight if you hadn't caught them."

I wasn't in the mood for smiling. "I'm Vallie Brown," I said as I pointed to Lucy and Davey. "Those are my sister and brother. They were playing tag and weren't paying attention. You're not from around here."

He smiled and I liked his smile. I also liked his brown eyes, sun-kissed face, and the way he fit into his clothes. "I'm visiting my aunt and uncle. You probably know Vern and Elsie Corbin as they go to this church. That is unless you are visiting also."

Vern and Elsie Corbin were relatively new-comers. They came from the city almost five years ago and had bought a big farm here.

I had to smile as I answered Ashton's question, "I wish I was. We live down the road about a half mile, and I come to the chapel every Sunday with my family."

"I saw you a few rows ahead of me. I guess my relatives must sit in the same place every Sunday. It seemed that everyone knew where to sit, although there were no names on the pews."

I nodded my head in agreement. "I guess it's a matter of habit." I pointed to Lucy and Davey busy pitching stones into the pond. "I have the task of watching them. That's the reason I made a fool of myself catching them before they upset the lemonade punch bowls."

He chuckled, "A fete of derring-do."

I ignored his remark and asked, "How long will you be staying?"

He removed his suitcoat."Sorry," he apologized. "It's getting too warm for a jacket."

"I don't mind," I said and I didn't. He looked even better without it.

"I'll be staying into July. I just graduated from the University down in Charlottesville. My parents thought an experience on a farm would be good for me before I settle into a real job."

"Why haven't you come to visit before now? At least, I've never seen you before or is it that you don't come to church when you're here?" Wasn't I bold?

He hesitated and offered a sly smile. "This is my first time here. I have other things to do in the summer. My parents thought I was too much into the fraternity way of life. Too many good times and not too serious about the keep-your-nose-to-the-grindstone way of life."

I had to laugh. "Mother thinks I'm a dreamer, but I know there must be a lot more to life. At least magazines make a person think there is. This church picnic must be boring to you."

Ashton didn't respond. He picked up a couple of flat stones and skipped them across the water.

Davey came running to where we stood. "Show me how to do that," he said as he tugged at Ashton's pant leg.

I brushed his hand away. "Davey that isn't polite."

Ashton laughed, reached down, swooped him up and pretended to throw him into the pond. Then he set him on his feet. "You can do it but it isn't easy. I'll show you how to hold the stone."

Lucy and I watched as the lesson began. Unfortunately, we were interrupted by the bell that announced the lunch was ready to be served.

"We have to go," I said. "You two young ones hold my hands until we get to our blanket." I looked over at the visitor, "It was nice to meet you, Ashton."

He gave a wide grin. "People call me Ash," he said.

"Ash," said Davey. "Why don't you come eat with us? Nora made some cherry tarts."

"Well, thank you, Davey. Maybe the next time as I have an obligation to my aunt and uncle."

Davey looked puzzled. "Is that bad?"

Ash laughed again. "I'll let you know after I eat."

I held the children's hands and headed to our spot. Ash's relatives were a distance away. Before they parted, he asked, "Shall I see you again?"

"Perhaps," I responded, trying to act nonchalant. And pointing south, "You can almost see my home from here. It's the big white farm house on the left."

Ash Corbin turned to find his aunt and uncle while I led the young ones to the tree where the blanket was spread. Luke and Mark were waiting.

"Who was that, Vallie?" asked Luke.

"His name is Ashton Corbin and he's visiting his aunt and uncle."

12

"Kind of fancy with a fancy name," Mark chimed in.

"He's going to teach me how to skip stones across the water," said a proud Davey.

Luke snickered. "Maybe he can teach me how to pitch a baseball."

"If he knows what one is," Mark replied. And then they both broke into laughter.

"Have your fun," I said as I looked in the direction he had gone. "He seems to be nice."

Yes, Ash Corbin seems very nice, indeed.

Chapter 3

On Mondays I helped Tizzie Nelson who lived in a small house on the Old Charles Town Road about a mile or so from ours.

Tizzie owned a lot of land, but she only took advantage of the area around her house, which was used for a big vegetable garden. The rest of the land was leased to other farmers. She had a few flowers, but as Tizzie said, "You can't eat flowers." In front of her house was a small stand where she sold vegetables during the summer and eggs when her chickens were laying. Tizzie Nelson was a practical woman.

I rode my gelding named Ches. He was the color of chestnuts and he had been my horse for six years. We had covered a lot of ground together. I could have walked the mile to the Nelson farm, but I had to ride by a rundown place that always gave me the jitters when I passed it. Three brothers, probably in their forties, lived there and would come out by the road to watch me go by. They were a motley looking trio with shabby clothes, shaggy hair, and long beards. Mother said they were harmless and to be nice because none of them were too bright. I'd press Ches into a gallop and wave my hand as I passed. That was as nice as I could be. They were smart enough to know that I went to Tizzie Nelson's every Monday morning. I tried to leave her house at different times, so I could evade them on my way back home. That didn't always work.

Miss Tizzie was waiting on the porch when I arrived. I put Ches in the small fenced in area where there was a troth of water and green grass for him to graze. It was another pretty June day. I always wore an old pair of Luke's pants when I rode Ches because it was more comfortable. I took off the pants and laid them across the saddle that I had lifted from my horse, and fluffed the skirt of my cotton work dress.

That part of Clarke County was rather flat with a lot of limestone rocks, so it took know-how and perseverance to keep a farm prosperous. Therefore, I had a lot of respect for this woman who had been a widow for fifteen years.

"It's time you got here, Girl," she greeted me. "I've got a lot for you to do."

Miss Tizzie always had a lot for me to do, but she paid me a dollar. Underneath her crusty exterior she had a kind heart. It took me a while to realize that. However, I had worked for her since I was fifteen and learned what to pay attention to and what to ignore.

For some unknown reason, Miss Tizzie seemed to be in a more compatible mood. "We've got some lifting to do today," said the thin wiry woman. "I got company comin'."

This announcement made my eyebrows raise as Miss Tizzie wasn't big on company.

15

"My cousin Eva Lou from down in southern Virginia will be here for a week, and if she hasn't changed she'll want the place spiffed up."

I made an inward groan. I don't think Tizzie Nelson ever got rid of anything. But, she was organized in her haphazard way of life.

"We'll start in the sitting room. You'll have to climb the ladder to the attic 'cause I'm gettin' too old to carry and climb at the same time."

The Nelson house consisted of a sitting room, kitchen, pantry and two bedrooms each one big enough for a twin bed, side table, chest of drawers, and a rocking chair. I never minded cleaning the bedrooms because the window let in sunlight and Miss Tizzie didn't pile them high with what I considered junk. The sitting room and kitchen were a different story. There were cubby holes all over that she stuffed full.

The ladder that led up to the attic was in one end of the kitchen. I wasn't sure how I was going to handle this, but I didn't have to worry because Tizzie Nelson was good at bossing me around. I carried piles of old newspapers and magazines, clocks, pots, pictures in frames, old toys and dolls, and even a rocking horse and spinning wheel up to the attic. By the time we were through my legs ached.

It was a time of nostalgia for Miss Tizzie. She would bring something to be stored and wistfully tell me who it had belonged to with a story attached. I learned a lot about Tizzie Nelson. She hadn't come from much, but she and her husband had worked hard together to make the farm go. Her one lament was that she didn't bear any children.

"That's the Lord's way, you know," she said with a sigh. I felt a twinge of regret, but I didn't pity her because that was not Miss Tizzie's way.

It was later than usual when I left. With all of the clutter packed away the house looked bigger and more comfortable. Even the outhouse got a good scrubbing with a bleach mixture, and I placed a small bouquet of roses in a canning jar on a ledge inside. When Miss Tizzie's cousin arrived two days from now, the whole place would look inviting. Although Miss Tizzie didn't say anything, she handed me an extra dollar and gave as big a smile as she was capable of offering. I left feeling that I had done a satisfactory job and had brightened her day.

It was getting around dinner time close to dusk when I headed Ches toward home. As I neared the House of Jitters, I saw one of the brothers standing in the middle of the road. That caused my heart to jump because I couldn't gallop past, so I slowed Ches to a steady walk. When I got to him the man grabbed the bridle causing Ches to start vigorously shaking his head, trying to break the hold. I patted his neck to reassure him all was okay, although I didn't know if it was.

"My brother's right sick, missy." There was a worried look on his weather-beaten face, but I wasn't going to get off my horse.

"What's the matter with him?" I asked.

"Don't know. He can't get outta bed."

I tried to act brave although my heart was pounding like a sledge hammer. "Well, you let go of my horse and I'll go tell my pa."

To my surprise the man let go of the bridle and stood back. I raced home, slid off Ches and went into the kitchen where Mother and Nora were busy. They both turned when I flew in the door.

"Land sakes, Vallie May! You look like you've seen a ghost," Mother exclaimed.

I could feel my face was flushed and my eyes felt as big as saucers. "No, but one of those Sugg brothers scared me to death. He says his brother's real sick and can't get out of bed. I told him I'd tell Father."

Mother wasn't too concerned. "We've got dinner ready, so we'll go on and eat. Your father can decide if we need to head over there. You wash up before the boys come in."

She put boiled potatoes in a big dish. "How is Miss Tizzie?" Mother asked.

"She's good," I said as I stood wiping my wet hands on a dish towel. "She's got a cousin coming to visit and I had to pile all of that junk she keeps up in the attic."

"I don't think Miss Tizzie considers it junk or she wouldn't keep it." Mother had a kind way of correcting us.

Loud laughter announced that my brothers were here for dinner, which meant my father was close behind. I settled Davey and Lucy in their chairs before I sat between them.

Midway through our meal Mother told Father about one of the Sugg brothers being sick. "Vallie said the one who stopped her looked upset and worried."

"We'd better go on over there once we're finished," said Father. "Those boys don't ask for help unless they need it."

When dinner was over, Mother and Father left for the Sugg place and I helped Nora clean up the kitchen. Luke and Mark took Davey and Lucy into the parlor to play a game of Crazy Eights.

When I went to bed my parents hadn't returned, but I felt good that I had given the message to Father. That also salved my guilt about being leery of the brothers Sugg.

Chapter 4

Tuesdays and Fridays were the days I rode Ches to the Lockwood estate. It was a good distance over off Clifton Road, and I would cut cross lots but it was still a ride. Both the horse and I had learned a good path to avoid bramble bushes, deep ruts and sink holes. At the Longmarsh Run I would let Ches drink before we crossed the shallow stream.

Miss Adelaide and I had an arrangement that if the weather was bad I wouldn't come. She had said that she understood and that was fine with her.

The day after I helped Tizzie Nelson, I was riding to Lockwood. The sky was overcast and Father said rain was likely. I rolled up a raincoat with a hood and tied it behind the saddle. If it was a heavy rain it would be some protection. On those days wiping down and currying Ches was a tiring task.

That morning after I put on the bridle and saddle I gave Ches a lump of sugar. "Let's go see Miss Adelaide," I said to him. I talked to my horse a lot and I'm not sure if that was because I liked the sound of my voice or the fact that he couldn't talk back.

It was a little after seven when I reached Lockwood. Miss Peg met me at the back door.

"They're in finishing their breakfast," she said. "You can go ahead and start upstairs."

I liked that idea because Mr. Lockwood wasn't too personable. He had been a lawyer in Berryville before he turned to running his estate. He was nice enough but he didn't talk much; I guess that was the lawyer training he'd had. There were a lot of people who liked to jump on your words and turn them around.

I took the broom, dust pan and cleaning cloth from the pantry and started for the wide stairs. I heard voices coming from the dining room before Peg came hurrying to the foot of the stairs. I stopped.

She motioned with a finger for me to come back down. "The Lockwoods want to talk to you," she said in a whispered voice.

That sent a jolt of discomfort from my head to my toes. What would they want to talk to me about? Had I done something wrong?

I left the cleaning supplies on the stair landing and followed Peg to the dining room. Miss Adelaide looked bright and cheery. Mr. Lockwood rose from his chair and pulled out another for me. I had never sat in the Lockwood dining room and wondered if they were going to blast me with some news that would cause me to keel over.

He began. "Miss Brown, I know you are aware that Mrs. Lockwood will soon need help when our baby arrives." I nodded. "What Mrs. Lockwood and I would both like is to have you consent to stay with us until Mrs. Lockwood is recovered."

21

It was fortunate that I was sitting or I may have swooned. Living at Lockwood? That meant being a nursemaid twenty-four hours a day. I wasn't sure I was up to that task. It took me a moment to answer until my speechlessness faded away. "I will have to check with my parents," I replied. "They will want to know what arrangements you are considering." Didn't I sound confident?

"Certainly," Miss Adelaide said with a comforting smile. "You can use the little room right off the front hallway. I will move into the room across the way. It should only be for a month. Once the baby arrives, I'll send word over to you. Mr. Lockwood is prepared to pay you a handsome sum."

I thought of asking what that handsome sum would be, but that might be impertinent. I did manage to ask, "When do you expect the baby to be born?"

"Both Dr. Hawthorne and Dr. Burke agree that it will be close to the first of July."

That would give me two weeks, I thought. It wasn't that I had big plans and it might get me out of the hot picking and canning of vegetables, and maybe Nora could help Miss Tizzie. I said I would talk with my parents. I knew a lot about babies as I had helped with Davey and Lucy when they were born.

The rain held off but the sky was getting dark when I left Lockwood. Pressing Ches into a trot we made it home just as a cloudburst sent driving rain. Ches walked into his stall where I threw him some hay. Then I curried him down and waited for the deluge to lessen. The respite gave me time to think about what the Lockwoods had proposed. I wasn't sure I would be comfortable with that arrangement. However, the thoughts of building up money in my piggy bank, and getting out of a vegetable canning mess were appealing.

Mother was in the kitchen when I went to the house. She turned to look at me when I arrived. "How was your day?"

"It was interesting," I replied.

"So was ours," she said. "We took George Sugg to Dr. Hawthorne. He had an appendicitis and it was close to breaking through."

That caused my eyebrows to raise. "No wonder his brother was worried."

"Dr. Hawthorne said that if it had burst George would most likely die from the poison, so both he and Dr. Burke operated right there at the Hawthorne House. It was too late to take him to the hospital in Winchester."

"Ugh!" I blurted out. "Is he going to be all right?"

Mother pulled open the oven door in the wood stove to check on the pot roast she was making for dinner. "Once he leaves the Hawthorne House, he'll have to come here until he can be on his own."

That wasn't good news. I wrinkled my nose. "Who's going to take care of him?" I asked.

"Don't worry," Mother said as she tested the roast with a fork. "That will be up to me, your father and the boys."

I let out an audible sigh of relief. Then I told her about the Lockwood proposal.

She shook her head. "I don't know. We'll have vegetables to put up."

I was sure she was going to throw up that barrier. "Nora will be here and the boys can help in the garden."

Her response was, "You can set the table. Nora went with Harold to buy chickens."

"Game chickens," I scoffed. My upbeat mood was deteriorating. The thoughts of George Sugg in the house and the task of canning vegetables were almost more than I could bear.

Mother was stirring gravy while I was setting plates on the table. Apparently, she had been thinking as she stirred because she said, "If the Lockwood baby comes in early July, the boys may have more time as it would be too early for the hay season. I'll ask your father about the Lockwood business when he comes in."

A pang of hope ran through me.

Chapter 5

Wednesdays and Thursdays were our usual days for laundry, and there were always baskets of coiled clothes. With eight people in the house, it seemed like a never-ending chore. Mother liked Ivory soap for our finer fabrics and Fels-Naptha for the barn clothes. She had to shave up the bar of soap with a knife, but Mother was convinced that Fels-Naptha worked the best to clean those dirty smelly clothes.

Nora was better at ironing than I was. We had two heavy irons that we heated on the wood stove, and it seemed I managed to singe something before we were done. That irked Mother because clothes and yard goods were expensive. I did my best to be careful, but sometimes I was just a klutz.

The Wednesday after the day I had the offer from the Lockwoods, Nora and I had two big washtubs set up on the back porch. We had done one load and were taking the pile of wet clothes out to the clothesline to hang.

There was a loud rumbling coming down the lane. Both Nora and I turned to see a farm truck approaching with Billy Wood driving. Billy Wood had never driven a farm truck that I knew of. In fact, there were few in our county.

Father and the boys came out of the barn, and I could see Mother peering out the kitchen window. Nora and I were curious enough that we left the wet clothes in their baskets as we stopped to watch.

"Billy, that's a right fine looking truck," was my father's greeting.

Billy Wood's freckled face blushed up to his dark-red hair. "Thank you, sir," he said. "I just bought it up in Winchester."

"It must have cost a pretty penny," said Father.

"Yes, sir, it did, but I figure it's gonna' pay for itself," replied Billy.

While Father and Billy were talking, Luke and Mark were busy looking the truck over. "Hey, Billy," Luke shouted. "Can we sit inside?"

"Sure. Go ahead." Billy hollered back.

When Billy turned, he noticed Nora and me standing and watching. With a shy smile and another flush to his face, he waved.

"He likes you, Nora," I said to her. "Billy is quiet, so I think he's too shy to let you know it. And, of course, he knows you and Harold are supposed to be semi-engaged. Go over and act like you're interested in his truck."

Nora always wanted to appear proper. "I'm not going to do that. It will look like I'm flirting."

"Come on," I encouraged. "I'll go with you."

"I don't know him that well," countered Nora.

"Certainly, you don't because you never let yourself get to know him." Wasn't I talking bold as though I knew the ways of the world?

To my surprise, Nora said, "All right. Let's go make fools of ourselves."

I had to admit it was a pretty truck. The cab was bright red with a large windshield, windows on the sides and one in the back. In the front were the engine, headlights and a shiny silver bumper. The spokes of the wheels matched the red of the cab. The bed of the truck was surrounded by wood slats. Billy showed us how he could open the gated back to carry animals.

Billy was so enthused showing us his brand new truck that his shyness disappeared. "Would you young ladies like to take a ride?"

I jumped at the offer. "Sure we would," I blurted out.

Nora, on the other hand, said, "We have those clothes to hang on the line."

"It'll be a short ride," said Billy.

After a moment of hesitation Nora agreed. I made sure that she sat in the middle next to Billy. He was stockily built. Nora and I were average in size, but she was finer boned than I. When we settled in, I could tell from the look on his face that Billy was pleased about the arrangement. After all, we were almost touching shoulder to shoulder.

We rode down the bumpy lane to the main road. The truck didn't ride much better than a wagon, but it was nice to sit inside on the black leather seat and watch the fields disappear as we passed. I had to wonder if it was like sitting in a train and watching different parts of the country, although I knew the train had to travel faster than this new farm truck.

Billy said he had plans to help out other farmers by bringing grain from town, and hauling animals off to the auction house. Of course he said he would have to charge a small fee. If Billy was a dreamer, he was putting his thoughts into action.

Nora surprised me again by getting into the conversation. "I think that sounds like a great plan," she said. "You could also bring groceries from town. Mother says she runs out of some supplies before it's time for Father to take the trip into Berryville."

Billy looked over and smiled at her. "I never thought of that."

When we arrived back home a short time later, I hopped out of the truck. Billy came around the front and held the door as Nora was climbing out.

"Thank you," she said. "I enjoyed that ride."

He smiled and in a quiet voice said, "How would you and Vallie like to go to the cinema in Berryville? *The Thief of Bagdad* is playing on Saturday night."

I was beginning to see more of Billy Wood than I thought existed. I was standing a few feet away. Nora looked over at me. "What do you think, Vallie?"

I knew Nora well enough to know that she wouldn't go by herself. A free night at the cinema sounded like a grand idea to me. And, the fact that

Nora would get to know Billy Wood better, and hopefully, ditch Harold gave me an inward smile.

"I'd love to go," I replied.

"Good," said Billy. I'll pick you up at six o'clock. Now I need to go talk to your father about a sow he has for sale."

Nora and I went back to hang up the wet clothes. "Do you think we should go? I don't know what Harold is going to say."

I hung up a bed sheet. "Don't go second guessing yourself, Nora. Harold will probably be off to some game chicken fight. Then he'll show up Sunday morning as the proper gentleman."

Nora didn't respond. Had I actually planted a seed of doubt in her mind or had she enjoyed the company of Billy Wood? Whichever, I didn't care, and a night at the moving picture show would get me out of the boredom of a lonely Saturday night.

Chapter 6

When Sunday morning arrived, I wasn't ready to get out of bed. My mind was still in a dreamy state of Douglas Fairbanks and Julianne Johnston running around Baghdad.

The cinema the night before had been a wonderful fantasy that took me out of the everyday world of farm life. The costume worn by the actors and actresses were lavish. I loved to sketch clothing, and I would doodle away any spare time I had to put on paper what I could picture in my mind. I wondered what it would be like to be a costume designer for a stage play or moving picture show. I'm sure that my family thought my designing was a big waste of time, and I guess I was a dreamer.

It was nine-thirty last evening by the time Billy Wood turned his new Ford truck onto our lane. He had been a perfect gentleman the whole night. He not only had paid for our tickets, but he had bought us popcorn and a glass of lemonade during the intermission.

There were some people there I recognized. A couple of girls I had gone to school with were now married and living in town. They were happy to see me and, naturally, asked what I was doing and did I have a boyfriend. All that small talk that young girls like to do. Of course, I had set them straight that Nora and I were only friends with Billy. I didn't want to fuel any rumors.

When Nora and I were getting into our nightgowns, she said, "I'm glad you talked me into going. Mother wasn't pleased because she thinks word will get back to Harold and cause a problem."

"What difference would that make? Maybe Harold needs to hear it, so he will realize that he needs to make a decision." I wasn't exactly sure how Nora felt about Harold. Was he more like an old shoe that was so comfortable a person didn't want to throw it away?

Nora didn't reply. She brushed her long brown hair. "You know, Vallie, I think Billy has a good plan for making his truck pay for itself. We had a nice talk while you were visiting with your friends. He thinks my idea of also carrying groceries is great."

"What do you think of Billy?" I had to ask.

"He surprised me. He has always been so quiet, I didn't realize that he is a deep thinker."

"You know that saying that 'still water runs deep'." I couldn't help but chuckle. "Harold just seems to float around on the surface."

Nora gave me a disgusted look. "I'm going to bed," she said and turned out the kerosene lamp.

It was time to get up. I could hear Lucy and Davey having a disagreement about something, so I hurried to get dressed. Nora was already up and helping in the kitchen by the time I got downstairs.

31

"How was your evening in town?" Mother asked.

Nora and I looked at each other. "I'm ready to run off with Douglas Fairbanks," I replied.

Nora smiled. "It was a grand evening, Mother. You and Father should go next week."

Mother shook her head. "Moving pictures are for young people. Your father and I are too settled in our ways."

Those words hit me like an electric bolt. Would I be feeling the same in my forties? I tried to put the words out of my mind as I went to get Lucy and Davey ready for church.

It was the usual Sunday morning of eating breakfast, dressing for church and climbing into the buggy while Luke and Mark were allowed to ride their horses.

When we arrived at Stone's Chapel, Harold and Nora were seated in their usual seats. I tried to be discreet as I looked to see if Ash Corbin was there. I saw Vern and Elsie Corbin but there was no sign of their nephew.

My hope sagged as Father seated us. I had so wanted to see Ashton Corbin again and so didn't want to sit through another Windy Wendell sermon. I didn't have a choice.

Chapter 7

Tizzie Nelson wasn't in sight the next day when I put Ches in the fenced in area. That was unusual because Tizzie always had her eye out for me to arrive.

I went up onto the creaky wood porch and knocked on the front door.

A refined little lady, who looked about the age of Tizzie, answered my knock.

"Hello," I said. "I'm Vallie Brown, and I help Miss Tizzie on Mondays."

"Oh, yes," she replied. "Tizzie told me you were coming. She isn't feeling well. I'm her cousin, Eva Lou. You come right in. Tizzie's in her bedroom."

I followed Miss Eva Lou to where Tizzie lay with a red face and looking like a used dishrag.

"Tizzie," Eva Lou announced. "The young girl is here to see if there is anything you need her to do."

Tizzie held up a hand for me to stop. "Don't come too close, Vallie, I think I caught that appendix stuff that George Sugg had."

"I don't believe you can catch that," I said, trying not to breathe. The whole room smelled like an outhouse.

I believe the sick woman thought my response impertinent because she frowned at me and was strong enough to say, "Well, he came by a day before he got sick. I've got the runs and nothing stays down. My whole body feels creepy."

That was no surprise to me.

"If you don't have any pain, you probably have what my mother calls a "stomach bug". How long have you been feeling bad?"

"Since Saturday, the day after Eva Lou came. She brought me the nicest crab salad. It's a shame she's run into this mess." Tizzie closed her eyes and I could see from her lifeless movement that she was worn out.

I didn't know about crab, but I did know that fish can go bad quickly. It seemed reasonable to me that if Eva Lou brought that salad on the train all the way from Norfolk that it could be Tizzie's problem, so I asked, "Miss Eva Lou, did you eat some of the salad?"

"Oh no, dear. I don't like crab," responded the demure Eva.

"Miss Tizzie, I think I should go home and get Mother. She's good at knowing what to do."

Tizzie waved a limp hand. "I don't want to put your mother out."

"She won't mind. Nora is home and she can make dinner for everyone." I didn't wait for her to respond.

I motioned Miss Eva Lou out of the room and into the kitchen. "I'm going home to get Mother," I told her. "She'll know what to do."

I could see relief wash over her worried face. "You go along, dear, and ask your mother to come. I don't know anything about taking care of sick people. Our servants always did it."

Servants? It was no wonder Miss Tizzie wanted the house spiffed up before Miss Eva Lou arrived. And, apparently, Miss Eva Lou had never emptied a chamber pot.

I went outside to where Ches was munching on hay. He turned his head and snorted. I put the bridle, blanket and saddle on Ches. I was sure he held a puzzled look so I explained. "We have to go home and get Mother," just as though he understood. Anyway, it made me feel better, and I put him in a gallop until we reached our lane.

Mother was in the kitchen when I hurried in. "Miss Tizzie is awful sick. Can you go and see?"

She wiped her hands on her apron. "What's the matter with her?"

"Her cousin is here, and she brought her some crab salad. I think it poisoned Miss Tizzie just like spoiled fish will do. I asked her cousin if she ate some and she said no. The whole place stinks." I could tell from the rise in my voice that I was anxious.

Nora came in from the living room. "I heard every word. Mother you go see what you can do. I'll take care of dinner."

I knew my mother well enough to know that she wouldn't refuse. For two reasons: one, because she was good with sick people and two, because she would feel it was her Christian duty.

She went into the pantry and placed supplies in a basket. She often laughingly called the pantry her apothecary.

When she was ready Luke hitched up the buggy. Mother drove the buggy while I rode Ches beside it. When we got to the Nelson house, Mother took in the basket while I took care of Ches and the buggy.

I do believe Miss Eva Lou was going to clap her hands and shout for joy when Mother met her on the porch.

It didn't take long for Mother to size up the situation. She unloaded her basket, ordered me to open a jar of chicken broth and told me to heat it up. Then she mixed baking soda and paregoric in a glass of water.

Mother said, "We'll start with a few drops at a time. If she can keep this down, it will only be a matter of getting some liquid into her."

Mother, Eva Lou and I were in the kitchen.

"What if she doesn't keep it down?" I asked.

"Then we'll have to get Dr. Hawthorne."

"Oh, dear. This does sound serious," murmured Eva.

I hoped my face didn't show my disbelief. I figured anyone with half a brain would realize this was a serious situation. Even the Suggs knew enough to get help for George.

Mother was more understanding than I. She took Miss Eva's delicate hand in hers. "You're not to worry. I'll stay right here with you." Then Mother looked at me. "You can start cleaning up after you fix Miss Eva a nice cup of tea."

She took Eva out to sit on the porch away from the stench inside.

I brewed the tea and took it out to the bewildered lady. If I was to start cleaning, I knew what to do, so I tied a dishtowel around my nose and mouth and went in to get the chamber pot.

It had a lid, for which I was grateful, but the big pot was almost full. If I could get to the outhouse without throwing up on the way, I could dump it in the hole and throw some lime down on it to help quench the smell.

Mother opened all the doors and windows. I took that nasty pot out by the well when it was empty, rinsed it out and then filled it with a bleach mixture. I had a stiff brush and scoured that white porcelain pot until it looked sparkling clean.

With all my heart, I hoped it would stay that way, but realistically I knew it wouldn't. I was becoming very good at feeling sorry for myself as I wondered if this way of life was to be my fate. It was a far cry from the models in the *McCall's* magazine.

The next day was my day to help at Lockwood. Mother knew that, so when Luke came by after dinner to see if we were all right, Mother told me to ride back home with him and she would stay all night.

I didn't think Miss Tizzie looked too much better, but Mother was encouraged because the runs had stopped. That was after I had to make another trip to the outhouse with a load of distasteful human matter. The house smelled better after I did a lot of cleaning and threw lots of peppermint sprigs around.

Luke brought fried chicken, cabbage salad, biscuits and bread pudding that Nora had made. Nora was a good cook.

Mother, Miss Eva and I ate dinner while Luke waited for me to ride home with him. He saddled Ches for me. When Mother and I had finished cleaning up from dinner, I was more than happy to be headed for home.

It was past dusk, but the moon was bright as Luke and I rode side by side.

"Mother told me to come back in the morning. She said that Miss Tizzie may need to see Dr. Hawthorne."

"You'll have to help with the milking first," I said.

"I know that," he answered.

We rode in silence until he asked, "Vallie, do you ever want to get away? You're older than me, and you're always reading those magazines."

I didn't hesitate with my answer. "I'd love to go to a big city, and I'd like to design all those pretty clothes I see in the magazines. I guess we all have dreams."

He thought about that. "Yeah," he said. "I'd like to be a baseball pitcher and play on one of those big city teams."

I looked over and smiled at him in the moonlight. "Maybe that's what life is, Luke. Just a lot of dreams."

When we got to our place we both noticed a flickering lantern light in the barn. Mark must have heard our approach because he came out of it in a rush.

"Luke, you'd better go in and help Father. There's a cow having a hard time trying to deliver a calf. You're better at it than I am."

Luke didn't ask any questions, if Father needed his help he knew better than to dawdle.

"I'll take care of the horses, Vallie. They can stay in the pasture for the night after I strip them down."

Those words were like music. "Oh, Mark, thank you. It's been a hard day and I'm worn out."

Nora was sweeping the kitchen floor when I went in the house. She looked as tired as I felt. For the first time, it dawned on me how much help Nora was. She had put Lucy and Davey to bed, made dinner for everyone and cleaned up the mess and dishes that always followed a meal. As I looked at her pretty smile, it made me twice resentful of Harold. My dear sister deserved better than that ingrate. Would she ever realize it?

"Mother isn't with you?" she asked.

I shook my head. "She decided to stay the night. Tizzie isn't doing well, but she's better. Her cousin is of no use at all. I don't think the woman had to do a day's work in her life."

"How long is she going to stay?" Nora asked.

I shrugged and took one of Nora's tasty cookies out of a jar on the table. "I don't know. Boy, these are good," I said as I bit into the one I held in my hand.

Nora hung the broom and dustpan on a hook near the pantry. "I wasn't sure they would be because I ran out of milk and filled in with sour cream."

She removed her soiled apron and took it out by the washtubs and tossed it in the dirty clothes basket.

I devoured another cookie. "Let's go to bed, Nora. I'm tired and so are you. If we stay here they'll come in from the barn and we'll end up making coffee and anything else they want."

She chuckled. "Vallie, you are a woman who thinks ahead. Let's hurry because we'll be up at the crack of dawn to fix breakfast. I hope Mother doesn't have to stay another day. She'll be exhausted."

She blew out the kerosene lamp and we went upstairs to our room.

"Mother told me to go ahead on to the Lockwood place as Miss Adelaide will be expecting me. I told her that I should stay home, but she insisted that I go. And, by the way, Luke is to go over in the morning. Mother said he may have to get Dr. Hawthorne."

I was in my nightgown and hopped into bed leaving Nora to turn down the lamp.

She pulled back her cover on her bed. "I hope Tizzie gets better fast. We'll have that George Sugg in the house in a few days. You know how Mother is, if she thinks she needs to care for Tizzie, she'll bring them both here."

That was the first time I ever heard Nora criticize Mother. However, I didn't chide her because I was dreading the same thing myself.

Chapter 8

I was still tired the next morning. Nora and I were up early to get breakfast on the table, and I had to get ready to go to Lockwood. I felt as though I was walking in a daze until I had a cup of coffee and that seemed to perk me up to a respectable gait.

I had to leave before Father and the boys came in after milking. I didn't want to leave Nora with the chores of feeding, getting the children settled, and cleaning up, but Mark was a good helper.

I knew Luke had to go to check on Mother and report back, which turned my mind to the Nelson place and I wondered if Tizzie was on the mend, or if Dr. Hawthorne was going to be summoned. That would disrupt the whole day. Truthfully, I didn't care as long as I didn't have to be in the middle of the muddle.

Father's words 'be home early' were in my head as I saddled Ches. I gave him a lump of sugar. "Ches, I think we are going to have an interesting day."

It was a pleasant June morning. I noticed the wild roses were about to bloom which would brighten up my ride. I loved the roses. In the fall I would gather rose hips so we could put them in our tea. Mother said they were supposed to be healthy, although didn't know why. She thought the hips helped to put some color in our cheeks. My mother had interesting ideas. Lockwood looked impressive as I rode up to the corral. I stepped behind a small storage building to slip off Luke's pants and put them with my saddle. They were great to protect my legs when I rode, but I didn't want anyone to know that I wore a pair of my brother's old pants.

I saw Alex Lockwood in the barn talking to Caleb Dunn, the foreman, and Jess Edwards his right-hand man. Because I'd heard gossip, it made me wonder if Mr. Lockwood knew much about farming, or if he just owned the big estate and they ran it for him. I guess there's no reason a retired lawyer can't become a farmer.

Those men and their wives were all friends, and it was because of Miss Adelaide's adventurous spirit that they all ended up married and living on the estate. It took me a while to sort out how it all came about. I'd love to hear that whole story. Someday, when I felt brave enough, I intended to ask Miss Adelaide to tell me in her own words how it all came to be.

But, right now I was hurrying on to the big house for a day's work.

I went up the back steps and into the kitchen where Miss Peg was busy at the stove. She turned to me with a welcome smile. "Good morning, Vallie. It's good you're here. Miss Adelaide isn't feeling well, so I'm getting a breakfast tray ready for her. You can take it up to her."

I'm not sure why, but that made me feel uneasy. "Is she just feeling tired? Mother says that the last couple weeks before the baby comes is a tiring time. She's not having any pains?"

"I don't think so. Do you know anything about the birthing process?" Peg asked.

"No, ma'am," I replied. "I saw my sister and brother after they were born. Of course, I've seen animals have their babies, and I figure it's not too much different. One big mess."

Peg laughed. "You're right about that. I don't want a mess like when Lottie's last one was born. Dr. Burke said it looked like a war zone, and he should know because he was an Army doctor."

"I don't know Dr. Burke. Mother has Dr. Hawthorne come. That's not often," I said.

"Your mother is good when people are sick."

Those words gave me a sense of pride because I knew that to be true. Mother would have been a good nurse.

Peg put a carafe of hot tea, scrambled eggs and toast on a warm plate, then she turned over a warm metal mixing bowl and put it over the plate. "This way it'll stay warm," she informed.

"Grab one of those linen napkins and take this tray on up to her."

I felt nervous. I had cleaned that bedroom, but never with anyone in it. I did as Peg ordered and went up the winding stairs.

When I entered the room after a polite tapping, she was sitting in a rocking chair in her

43

robe and slippers. I had to admire her robe because it was light and lacy. Her embroidered slippers matched the blue of her robe. Even though she was big and round with a baby coming, Miss Adelaide liked to be fashionable.

"I'm sorry to hear you're not feeling well," I said as I placed the tray on a side table by her chair.

"I'm glad you're here, Vallie. I believe it's time for me to move into the room downstairs. You can empty the drawers and linen closet and take those goods down. I'll have Peg tell Mr. Lockwood to have the men come to help move furniture."

I was happy that responsibility was up to Peg because I surely didn't want to talk to Alex Lockwood if I didn't have to. I just never felt up to his station in life.

"What did your parents say about you coming to stay here until I'm back on my feet after the baby comes?" she asked.

I was removing the metal bowl that covered her plate of food. "They both agree that it will be all right because it will be before the haying season and the tomatoes and corn ripen."

She chuckled. "We farmers live by seasons, don't we? However, I am very pleased to know you will be here. Now, I hope I can keep this down."

"Miss Peg gave me this bell. She says to ring it whenever you need something." After placing the bell on the table beside her, I left the room to take up my usual tasks.

I was dusting the upstairs sitting room when I heard Jess Edwards' booming voice, which was as big as he was coming, from the kitchen. "Hey there, Peg of my heart. I hear you have some furniture to be moved."

"Don't you be dragging in any dirt on them cowboy boots," Peg answered.

I chuckled to myself because I was getting used to their good natured banter. I liked Miss Fannie's husband.

I heard him bound up the stairs and rap on Adelaide's door. She told him to come in. I didn't mean to eavesdrop, but I could hear their whole conversation.

"Hop into my arms, Addie, and I'll carry you to your new perch," Jess kidded her.

"Jess Edwards, can't you ever be serious?" was her mild admonishment.

"I leave that up to Caleb. He likes to worry. What do you need moved?" Jess asked.

"Well, you can't do it yourself."

"I'm sure of that," he answered. "But, Caleb wants to know so it won't ruin his plans for the afternoon."

"How's Fannie? I haven't seen her for a few days," Adelaide lamented.

"She's been staying close to the cabin until the baby comes. I'll tell her you asked," he said. "Lottie's been by a couple times and brought dinner. She said she knew Fannie wouldn't feel much like cooking."

"Lottie is such a good person," Miss Adelaide said. Then she told him what she wanted done. Miss Adelaide was an organized woman.

I had told my loyal horse that it was going to be an interesting day, but I didn't know how interesting until I got home.

As usual at that time of day, Mother and Nora were in the kitchen getting the evening meal prepared. Nora left the small table where she was pealing carrots and whispered, "Miss Tizzie is in the hospital in Winchester, and Miss Eva Lou is sitting in the parlor."

I looked at her with a blank stare. I knew what that meant. Nora and I would have to sleep on cots on the screened in porch upstairs.

Nora must have read my thought because she said, "Mother couldn't very well leave her there alone at Tizzie's place."

I knew that was true, but it didn't mean I liked the idea of giving up my room. "How long is she going to be here?" I whispered back.

"She is going to be with relatives in Washington, so Luke will take her up to the Bluemont station to get the train."

"Girls, get busy," Mother said, which meant our private whispered conversation was over.

I washed my hands and started setting the table. I figured one night on the cot wasn't so bad, it could have been worse.

Mother had prepared a fried chicken dinner, which was delicious. Miss Eva Lou praised her to high heaven not only for the succulent dinner, but for rescuing her from the Nelson place. Mother deserved to be commended for her good deeds, although I was sure she would feel uneasy. Mother would consider her good deeds to be doing the Lord's work.

After dinner, Nora took Miss Eva Lou upstairs to our room, where she settled in for the night. I helped Mother clean up the kitchen after I put Lucy and Davey to bed.

"Vallie," Mother said. "You are to ride up with Luke tomorrow when he takes Eva to the train. She will be more comfortable and so will he."

"Why can't Nora go? She's better at conversation than I am." It was a long ride in the buggy up to the station on the mountain. Then I remembered. "Doesn't Mr. Marks drive a big car up there from Berryville?"

Mother turned from what she was doing and placed her hands on her hips. "Miss Vallie May, I am not going to put that little lady in a car with strangers."

When she used both of my distasteful names and put Miss in front of it, I knew that was the end of my complaining.

After I finished and went upstairs, Nora was already lying on her cot.

"Mother says I have to go with Luke tomorrow." I was still aggravated.

"I know." She chuckled. "Aren't you the lucky one?"

"I don't think it's funny," I said.

"In case you've forgotten, tomorrow is wash day. You'll miss most of it."

I shrugged. "I think I'd rather do that."

Nora wasn't fooled. "Hah! I know that's not true. You hate wash day. Take some of those sketches you do and show them to Eva Lou. She looks like a prissy lady who would gush at the clothes you design."

"They're just for fun," I said. "Luke and Mark always joke about them."

"What do boys know?" she said. "Vallie, you have a talent."

That was the first time I could remember that Nora sincerely complimented me on my drawings. My sour mood changed and I went to sleep feeling encouraged. The buggy ride with Eva Lou and Luke didn't sound so bad after all.

Chapter 9

The next morning after a filling breakfast, Luke loaded Miss Eva's carrying case into the rear of the buggy. The sky was overcast, but Father said, "Keep in mind that the weather on the mountain can be different, so take the two umbrellas." The buggy had a canopied top. If it was a light rain, we would stay dry. I took my canvas cover that I used when I rode Ches in the rain just to be on the safe side. I didn't like the feel of wet clothes.

Mother sent a lunch with Miss Eva to eat on the train. I packed a sandwich and apple for Luke and the same for myself because I knew we would be hungry before we returned. I also put a jug of water in the buggy.

When we were set, the whole rest of the family came out to wave goodbye. Luke tapped the reins and we started the long trip to the Bluemont station, which I figured was about twenty miles. I had only been there a couple of times, and that was to see relatives off as my family was not one to travel.

When we reached the town of Berryville, Miss Eva had Luke stop and park the buggy on Main Street. Then she gave him money and told him to go into Coyner's and buy a box of Fannie Farmer chocolates for Mother, which he did. Chocolates were a rare treat in our house because they were expensive.

It appeared that Miss Eva had plenty of money and a gift of gab. I didn't have to worry about not being the best conversationalist. When there was a lull, I pulled out my drawings from a case I carried after Eva said she would be interested in seeing them.

"It's something I do in my spare time," I said to her. "Mostly I draw my designs in lead pencil. I tried to color them, but the crayons were too bulky and waxy," I explained.

Eva seemed quite interested. "But you have colored these few pages," she remarked.

I smiled a shy smile. "Those I did with colored pencils. I saw them at Mr. White's general store. He said they were brand new on the market." I felt my face flush. "I probably shouldn't have spent the money."

"Nonsense. These are designs that need color to show them off. Do you mind if I keep a couple? I do admire fashion."

I was more than glad to let her take what she wanted. To have someone admire my drawings gave me a sense of pride. Mother would probably think that was sinful.

Before I realized it, we were going around the horseshoe curve in the road in Pine Grove and headed up the mountain to the train station.

Miss Eva was not as helpless as she would have us believe. She marched into the small station, ordered her ticket and ordered a young employee to take her bag to the baggage platform. Then he was to put it in the second passenger car on the seat in the second row. Luke and I heard the conversation.

"I plan to sit next to the window and I don't care to have anyone sit next to me," Eva Lou said to the wary young man.

A moment of hesitation before he answered, "Yes, ma'am. What if there is someone in that seat?"

"Well, move them on, young man. Do as I say." Then she turned to Luke and me. We had been waiting to be sure all went well. "I thank you and your people for all of your help. I shall be living in Washington from now on. You and all of your family will be welcome to visit any time you come into the city. I have left my address with your mother."

"Yes, ma'am," Luke said.

I just smiled. The likelihood of visiting Miss Eva Lou was remote.

Miss Eva Lou flitted her hand. "Go along now," she said.

We were properly dismissed and both of us were happy to be on our way back home.

"Boy, she is a strange old woman." Luke said.

I nodded my agreement. "But, you have to admit she was interesting."

"I guess," he answered and tapped the horse with the reins to get started.

Chapter 10

The week had flown by. I didn't go to Lockwood on Friday because Miss Adelaide had sent word by a hired man that she wanted me to come on Monday ready to stay at the big house.

Fortunately, it worked out well as Tizzie Nelson was in the hospital, so I wouldn't have to be at her place on Monday. The hired man didn't say the baby was here, but l was sure it meant it was on its way. My hope was that the baby would arrive before I got there.

Also, Dr. Hawthorne told Mother that George Sugg could be released Monday. Mother thought the Lord was working in her favor, maybe He was but He was also doing me a favor. I didn't want to be here when George arrived.

Nora and I cleaned out a small room on the first floor that Mother used as a work room. Luke and Mark brought one of the cots from the upstairs screened porch. I vowed I would never sleep in that cot again even though we covered it with a rubber sheet. The sheet was one Mother kept after Davey was born.

We followed her instructions and the cozy room looked inviting when we finished.

Today was Sunday and we went through the usual routine. I hoped Reverend Stephens wasn't as longwinded today because I wanted to get home and pack what I needed for Lockwood. The thought of staying at that grand house gave me butterflies in my stomach. I had mixed feelings about going. On the other hand, when I thought of George Sugg moving in, it firmed my resolve that Lockwood was worth a few anxious moments.

We were later to arrive at Stone's Chapel than our usual time. Most of the members were already seated. However, our pew was waiting for us with Harold and Nora already there. If Ashton Corbin was here, it would be embarrassing to walk down the aisle with those seated watching the parade. Father went on ahead and Mother poked me in the back to start on down. Uneasy as I felt, I went forward and the rest of the family fell in line.

I tried not to look right nor left. Unfortunately, I caught a glimpse of Vern and Elsie Corbin. Sitting with them was Ashton. I wanted to turn and run out the door or drop through the floor. Instead, I continued to walk to the pew with my face burning like a hot poker. Why did seeing Ash affect me so? I knew Nora saw my embarrassment and patted my hand when I sat down.

Naturally, Windy Wendell gave his long sermon. My mind was so filled with the upcoming week I didn't even pay attention.

Before I realized it we finished the last hymn and it was time to leave. I hoped the Corbins would be gone by the time we reached the outside. That was not the case. Vern and Elsie were talking with a group of people and so were my parents.

I stood apart wishing they would soon leave for home. As I waited at the side, Ash came over.

"Hello, Vallie." I liked the sound of his voice.

"Hello," I said. "I'm surprised to see you. I thought maybe the country life was not to your liking."

He laughed. "I'm stuck. Did you look for me last week?"

"Why should I?" Wasn't that a stupid remark?

"I'd be pleased if you did," he said.

"I had better things to do." And gave a coy smile.

By now I could feel my heart beating so hard I thought he might hear it. I didn't like this feeling and wondered why he affected me so. Probably because he had gone to college. I wasn't used to people of that class.

"Are you busy this afternoon?" he asked.

"Yes," I replied like a fool. "I have to be gone for a couple of weeks and I have to pack."

"Are you going on a trip?"

Honesty got the better of me, and I answered, "No, Mrs. Lockwood's baby is due to arrive, and I'm going to stay at Lockwood to care for her until she's back on her feet."

A big smile appeared on his pleasing face. "My aunt and uncle are friends of the Lockwoods. Perhaps I'll see you there. I'm glad I saw you, Vallie," he said. Then he turned to catch the buggy as the Corbins were on their way.

My family was waiting, so I climbed in ours. "Who was that young man?" Mother asked.

"He's a nephew of Mr. and Mrs. Corbin," I replied.

"Oh, yes," she said. "I remember he was here for the picnic. He appears to be a nice young man."

I nodded my agreement and did my best to act nonchalant. I did not want to show how very nice I think he is.

At home I was packing my valise when I heard a quiet tap on my bedroom door. When I opened it, there stood Lucy with a downcast expression on her sweet round face.

"Come in, Lucy. You can help me. Why do you look so sad?" I kissed her cheek.

"Are you going away for a long time?" she said.

"Not so very long," I answered.

"Who's going to put us in bed and read us stories or tell us nursey rhymes?" I could tell she was near tears, so I gave her a reassuring hug.

"Mother and Nora will be here, or maybe you can get Mark to tell you stories. He's good at that."

Lucy shook her head. "Mother and Nora are always too busy, and Mark can't tell stories as good as you."

I did feel sorry for her as I knew that time of evening was always a busy time. "I have to go and help Mrs. Lockwood because they will have a new baby. When I come home, I'll read a lot of stories and we can recite nursery rhymes together. You know a lot of them. Maybe you can teach them to Davey."

This brought a smile. "Am I smarter than Davey?"

"You're older than Davey. You'll have to be the big sister while I'm away." I hoped my words would make her feel better.

Apparently they did because she gave me a hug. She passed Nora on the stairs, and I heard Lucy say, "I'm going to teach Davey nursery rhymes."

Nora came into the room. "What was all that about?"

"Lucy was sad that I wouldn't be around to tuck her in and tell bedtime stories. Either you or Mother should make it a point to fill in while I'm gone."

Nora didn't comment. She sat on the side of her bed. "Do you need help?"

I shook my head. "I'm almost through. I'm nervous about going."

Nora smiled. "I would be too. Miss Adelaide must like you and the way you work."

I shrugged. "I guess."

Nora sat for a quiet moment before she said, "When Harold went to get the buggy, Billy Wood came to me and asked if I would like to go to a barn dance on Saturday night."

I dropped the skirt I was folding and stared at her. "What did you say?"

"I was so dumbstruck, I didn't know what to say. After all, I was waiting for Harold."

56

I was glad. "I didn't know Billy had that much courage. You should go."

"I don't want to cause a scandal. Mother won't be pleased, but I told Billy I would have to think about it."

"And…"

"And he said he had to come to see father on Wednesday and I could give him an answer then." Nora looked tentative.

"You should go, Nora," I encouraged. "Harold does what he pleases, and expects you to be here at his beck and call. I like Billy. You going with Billy may spur Harold into action." Although I doubted it.

Nora thought about it. "Maybe I will. It would be more fun than sitting here." She rose from the bed. "We're going to miss you around here."

"I hope it will only be for a couple of weeks. At least, I'll miss George Sugg."

Nora laughed. "I wish I could go with you. We'll probably have Tizzie Nelson here, also, once she's out of the hospital."

That was an unpleasant thought. "Mother can move the other cot down and put them both in that cozy room. Wouldn't that start tongues wagging?"

Nora chuckled. "Vallie, you'd better not let Mother hear you say that."

After picking up her knitting bag she left the room. Did I detect a spring in her step? I smiled to myself and finished packing what I thought I would need. For sure I would take my paper and colored pencils for when I had some quiet moments. Drawing my sketches while letting my mind wander were the best relaxation ways I knew.

That evening we all sat around the long oak table. While Father said the blessing there wasn't a sound to be heard. However, the minute he was through it was like the dam had broken loose. Everybody had something to say. On Sundays we ate earlier because Mother always put a roast and vegetables in the oven before we went to church. I liked our Sunday dinners.

Toward the end of the meal Mother told Luke and Mark they would have to take care of Tizzie's place. "Vallie is going to be gone, and with Tizzie in the hospital someone has to look out for her."

"Why do we always have to watch out for others?" complained Luke.

"Yeah," Mark chimed in. "We'll probably have to haul George Sugg in here."

"That's enough, boys," said Father. My father was a man of few words.

Mother took over. "They are our neighbors and neighbors watch out for each other. And, when Mr. Sugg comes to stay with us, we will treat him as a guest."

"I'd like to be treated like one," quipped Luke, which gave him and Mark a good laugh. I saw a half-smile on Father's face, but Mother just shook her head.

When Nora and I went to bed, it gave my heart a thud when I realized that I wouldn't be waking up in our comfy room for a few weeks. It was a fleeting sense of loss. I vowed to myself that I would make the adjustment with a sense of adventure. A person can learn a lot by living and listening to others.

Chapter 11

The next morning Luke had the buggy ready. Mark rode Ches. I wasn't going to leave my animal friend behind, and Mark could ride back with Luke in the buggy. It would give them some brotherly time together.

Because of the buggy we had to take the long way around, which meant taking Allen Road to Lewisville Road, then on to Clifton.

I had mixed feelings about leaving. My absence meant more work for Mother and Nora. George Sugg would be an extra burden, not to mention Mother's concern about Tizzie Nelson in the hospital.

On the other hand, I didn't know exactly what I was getting into at Lockwood. I didn't even know if Miss Adelaide's baby had been born. With all my heart, I hoped so. The moans, groans and shrieks of a woman in labor did not appeal to me.

"What are you thinking about?" asked Luke. You're awful quiet."

"Wondering what I'm going to find at Lockwood, and hoping Mother doesn't overwork herself."

Luke shrugged. "You know how Mother is. She'd save the world if she could."

"You and Mark had better pitch in and help, especially at keeping an eye on Lucy and Davey."

"Pa keeps us busy enough around the farm," he replied with a hint of irritation. "Besides, you didn't have to come over here."

I knew he was right, and it wasn't my place to carp at my younger brother. "I'm sorry, Luke. I know you and Mark both have a lot to do."

"That's okay," he said. Then he changed the subject. "I saw that Ash fellow talking to you after church. Does he seem to be a decent sort?"

Those words brought a pleasant thought to my mind and I couldn't help but smile. "He does, but I think he's wiser to the ways of the world than I am."

Luke chuckled. "A lot of people are wiser to the world than we are."

We heard Mark holler, "Lockwood's in sight. I'm going to go on ahead to take care of Ches. Where does he go, Vallie?"

"In the corral by the barn," I hollered back. "I'll check on him when Luke and I get there."

Mark trotted Ches by the buggy. I watched them go with a proud feeling for both my brother and my horse.

Luke guided his horse up the lane to where it forked. He took the one to the left which led to the rear of the big house. I could see Mark latching the corral gate before he attended to the bridle and saddle.

"Go ahead onto where Mark is," I told Luke. "I want to be sure Ches is settled before I go into the house."

Luke drove the buggy to the corral, where he and I got out. Caleb Dunn, the foreman, came out of the barn. He waved a welcome.

"Hey, Luke. It's good you brought your sister. Plenty of excitement up at the house."

"Hi, Mr. Dunn," said Luke. "We got word that she was needed."

Caleb smiled. "You'll have your work cut out for you, Miss Vallie. There's two babies up there."

"Did Miss Fannie have her baby, too?" I questioned.

Caleb's smile widened. "No, the Lockwoods have twins, a boy and a girl."

No wonder Miss Adelaide wasn't feeling well the last time I was here, I thought. And, there was another fleeting thought of what have I got myself into?

Peg came out onto the back porch when she heard the buggy.

"I saw you and your brothers come in," she said. "I've made a couple sandwiches and some cookies for the boys for a lunch on the way home."

Mark jumped out of his seat and onto the porch before I could say thank you.

"That's right nice of you, ma'am." I heard him say. "Luke and I don't seem to have any bottoms to our stomachs."

Peg laughed as she handed Mark the two bags of lunch. "I remember how it is with growing boys," she said.

Luke remained seated. He tipped his hat to Miss Peg, and I marched up the steps to stand by Mark with my tote bag in hand. "You'll have to get my big bag out of the buggy," I ordered him.

He just chuckled. "Oh, that's right. Guess the sound of food got in the way."

Mark took the two lunches, handed them up to Luke and returned with my bag. "Need anything else?" he asked.

"Can the boys help you with anything, Miss Peg?" I thought she deserved some reward.

She shook her head. "The main thing is they brought you. We've got plenty to do."

My brothers left and I followed Peg into the kitchen. "You go ahead and put your things in the room you'll be using. The babies arrived just after midnight. Miss Adelaide is plum tuckered out. When you get your things put away, I'll go over what's expected of you."

I carried my belongings to the small room and put away what I had brought. There were hooks on the wall where I could hang some clothing, shelves for toiletries, and a lovely corner desk for my sketching pads and pencils. How much free time I would have was a question, and one I couldn't answer. The big house was quiet. It was too quiet for me as I was used to the constant hub-bub that was our everyday life on the farm. But, there's nothing wrong with quiet.

Chapter 12

It was three days later when I saw Dr. Hawthorne drive up the lane in his Ford Tin Lizzie, as people liked to call the popular and practical automobile.

I felt relief. My responsibilities were to answer the cries of the babies, change their diapers and take the little bundles to Miss Adelaide for feeding.

The babies were born three weeks earlier than expected, and it appeared they could have used those weeks to put on some weight. They were tiny, pink and what my mother would call, scrawny. At first I was afraid to handle them because they seemed so fragile, but the more I held them the more comfortable I felt. Miss Adelaide seemed as cautious as I was.

Alex, named after his father, appeared stronger than his twin sister. The babies looked nothing alike. Alex was bald and Anna had a head full of dark hair. It was too soon to know what the color of their eyes would be. In fact they didn't open their eyes much, and they did sleep a lot. It seemed they had their own interior clocks when it came to feeding. Alex would wake up first. Then Anna would stir when I placed him back in the cradle.

Miss Adelaide was trying to nurse both of them. I wasn't sure that was a good idea because maybe they weren't getting enough nourishment. That's one reason I was relieved to see Dr. Hawthorne, and the second reason was because Miss Adelaide didn't seem happy. Of course, these were not anything that I thought I could discuss with Peg. After all, I was eighteen and what did I know about birthing babies. However, I did remember my mother cooing and chirping like a bird when Lucy and Davey were newborns.

Dr. Hawthorne was a big man with a big voice. I heard him the moment he came in the foyer. Miss Peg had gone to the door to meet him.

"I'm certainly glad to see you," I heard her say.

"No doubt," he replied. "I would have come yesterday, but I gave one more day in case something went wrong. That most likely happens on the third day, so I gave myself one more day to right the wrong. How are things going?"

Peg lowered her voice so I couldn't hear what she told him. At that point I heard Alex cry. After only three days, I could discern the difference in the cries of the two. It was my job to get him to his mother, so I went across to Miss Addie's room and found Dr. Hawthorne and Miss Peg already there.

I changed the wet diaper, bundled him in a blanket and took him to his mother. Dr. Hawthorne intercepted and took Alex from my arms. He laid the crying, scrawny baby on the bed and unwrapped the blanket. After a quick exam of the infant, he looked over at me. "What do you think? Does he seem to nurse well?"

He was asking me? Why wasn't he asking Peg or Miss Adelaide? Because Peg wasn't around for feeding and it was like Miss Adelaide showed little interest. Dr. Hawthorne was quick to size up a situation.

I hesitated before I answered, "Baby Alex seems stronger and ready to feed. I can't say the same for Anna." I did hold concern for Anna because her cry was weak and she was kind of blue looking. Those observations were something else I kept to myself. However, I did keep her wrapped in double blankets.

Alex was still crying. The doctor picked him up and handed him to Miss Addie. I moved around Dr. Hawthorne, wrapped the baby back in his blanket and helped Miss Addie get situated to nurse the hungry infant.

What I didn't expect was that Miss Addie burst into tears for some unknown reason. Peg left the room. Dr. Hawthorne stood there by the bed.

Through her tears, she said, "I'm doing the best I can."

My heart felt like it would break. This was not the Adelaide Lockwood I knew. What happened to the vibrant, happy, in-charge Miss Addie?

Dr. Hawthorne looked as though this was not unusual. He offered a sympathetic smile. "Certainly you are. Sometimes after a baby is born there is a period of let-down. You have been waiting months, all of a sudden the waiting is over. It takes time for the mind and body to adjust. In your case, Adelaide, you have to adjust to two babies instead of one."

He pulled a straight chair closer to the bed and sat down. The baby kept nursing and Miss Addie kept shedding silent tears. I stood near Anna's cradle, fearing the tenor of the room was going to disturb her.

After a few quiet minutes, Alex finished nursing and was sound asleep. That was a signal for me to move into action. I put Alex back in the cradle and made sure Miss Addie was comfortable.

Dr. Hawthorne sat writing notes in a small notebook. "I'll tell you what I'm going to do," the doctor said. "I'm going to leave some powder for Peg to fix in your tea to help cure the blues. It won't hurt the babies."

He rose from the chair and came to where the two babies lay in a large wooden cradle. One baby at each end. He picked up the sleeping Anna and carried her to the bed.

I wasn't sure what I was supposed to do, so I followed behind him. He unwrapped the baby, who was now starting to waken. I stood watching as he examined the tiny figure. Then he shook his head and turned to me. In a confidential voice he said, "This little girl is fragile. Keep her as warm as you can." He smiled at me. "Kind of like the baby chicks who aren't ready to leave the nest."

Anna was awake and it was time to take her to her mother. Miss Addie had recovered from her bout of tears, but her smile was not there when I settled the baby to be fed.

Dr. Hawthorne spoke to Miss Addie. "Adelaide, I'm going to set up a feeding schedule.

For a few days, we're going to take some of the burden off you by alternating the babies with nursing and goat's milk. They both need to start putting on some weight and the goat's milk will be easier on their stomachs. That will give you time to get back on your feet."

Miss Addie nodded.

"I'll talk with Peg and Miss Vallie, here, and we'll get back on the right track."

That sounded good to me because I was beginning to feel as down as Miss Adelaide looked.

Dr. Hawthorne picked up his medical bag. "I'll be back in a week unless you need me before then," he said and left the room.

Anna had finished nursing and I was swaddling her back in her double blankets before placing her in the cradle. I made Miss Addie comfortable and then went to the kitchen where Dr. Hawthorne was writing down his instructions. He, Peg and I sat at the small oak table.

"We've got to perk this place up," he said. "It might take some time, but once our lady gets some strength back, I believe she's going to be fine. As for the babies, they're going to need some extra care."

I didn't think that sounded good and the concern must have shown on my face because Peg said, "We'll do our best, Vallie. If we need extra help, I'll talk with Mr. Alex."

Dr. Hawthorne shook his head. "You two ladies see if you can handle it. It's a matter of following this schedule. The less people involved is better for the babies, less germs to spread. And keep visitors away for the next week. Either Dr. Burke or I will be available if you need us before I return."

After the doctor left Miss Peg and I went over what he had ordered. She would take care of the medicated tea and boil the goat's milk. I would switch the babies with nursing and bottle feeding. I wrote down my own schedule so I could keep it straight. Wouldn't it be wonderful if I could bottle feed one baby while Miss Addie was nursing the other? It would give me more time to rest. I was already tired.

As for Miss Adelaide, we were to continue as we had before the babies came. In Dr. Hawthorne's words, "Don't pussy-foot around."

Peg sent me down to Miss Lottie's to borrow baby bottles if she had any. Then I was to go to the barn and ask Mr. Dunn to have a hired man bring up a jar of goat's milk. Just getting out of the house and feeling the warm sun gave me a spring in my step. The thought jumped into my mind that this was what Miss Adelaide needed. There was no reason she couldn't get out of that stuffy room and sit on the front porch to have her tea.

Neither Miss Lottie nor Miss Fannie had come to the house. They said they wanted Miss Addie to have a week to recover. Miss Addie was going to need more than a week, but on my walk to the Dunn house I felt more encouraged.

Chapter 13

Nora Brown sat in front of the dresser mirror trying to make her hair do what she wanted it to do. She missed Vallie, but it was kind of nice to have their bedroom to herself. Nora was nervous. She had accepted Billy Wood's invitation to go to the barn dance against her mother's wishes.

Her mother was sure it would create un-wanted gossip. After all, wasn't Nora semi-engaged to Harold? Vallie could be blamed for making Nora think deeply about her relationship with Harold, and the result of her searching her brain was that she may be spinning her wheels waiting for Harold to make some kind of commitment. Going to the dance with Billy might just be the catalyst to move Harold into action.

Nora liked Billy. However, she felt a stab of guilt that her reason for going to the dance was to spite Harold. It was too late now.

She gave one more cursory glance in the mirror and pronounced herself ready to go.

Mother had put George Sugg on the down-stairs back porch. It was comfortable enough and convenient to give him the care he needed, which wasn't too much. Mostly, it was to feed him well so that he could build up his stamina to return to his hovel of a home. Nora was afraid that he might like being waited on so much that he would want to stay. Her mother was a good nursemaid along with all of the other duties of the house. She wouldn't let Nora care for George. That was left up to the boys when they were needed and that was fine with Nora.

Tizzie Nelson was still in the hospital. Mr. Brown was concerned about Tizzie's place, so Nora and Luke were elected to go twice a week to keep it in shape.

Nora heard Billy drive up in his new red farm truck. It would be around ten o'clock when they would return from the dance and coming home in the truck after dark was more appealing than coming home in a buggy.

Nora answered the door when she heard Billy knock. He smiled a shy smile. "Hi, Nora."

"Hi Billy, I'm glad you're here. I just need to pin on my hat and I'm ready to go."

Mrs. Brown must have heard them because she came into the parlor from the kitchen. "Hello, Billy."

"Good evening, Mrs. Brown," he replied.

"What time can we expect you to be home?" she asked.

"The dance will be over around nine, but we can be back earlier if you want," Billy said.

Nora's mother shook her head. "No, that isn't necessary. Have a good time."

Nora could tell in the tone of her mother's voice that she still wasn't pleased with her daughter's decision. Nora hoped Billy didn't pick up on it.

When they got to the truck, Billy opened the door for her. She stepped up on the running board and swung into the passenger's side of the cab.

Billy looked over at her with a wide smile. "You look very nice," he said.

Nora felt her face blush. She thought Billy looked very nice also, but she didn't say so. "Thank you," she replied. He was wearing a pair of tan slacks and a green plaid shirt. The colors matched well with his red hair and ruddy complexion.

Nora didn't have time to sew a new dress, so she wore her prettiest blue-checked cotton dress with lace on the bodice.

The place for the barn dance was about three miles away on the big farm. The barn was old, but sound. Only the first floor was used for freshened animals and their newborn offspring. The top floor, which once held hay, was now the dance floor. There was a raised platform where the four piece band sat. The group consisted of a fiddler, guitarist, bass violinist and a drummer. The guitarist was also a caller for square dances. They played a variety of music much to the delight of the dancers so they could pick and choose.

It wasn't long before Nora discovered the shy and retiring Billy Wood was a different person when it came to dancing. He knew them all. It was not the same for Nora, so she said she had no problem sitting out if a square needed another couple. There were plenty of girls who wanted Billy for a partner.

"Go ahead, Billy," she encouraged. "They need you."

"It isn't polite of me to leave you sitting by yourself," he protested.

The former hay mow was lit with big kerosene lamps. "In this dim corner no one is going to notice," Nora said. "Hurry out there so they can get on with the dance."

"You're sure?"

"I'm positive," she said.

Then he really surprised her by giving a quick kiss on the cheek. That wasn't the only surprise because Nora found that she liked that quick brush of his lips on her skin. He watched as the caller put the dancers through a routine. Billy was good. It was no wonder the girls wanted to dance with him.

When it ended, he came to her, offered his hand and said, "Let's get a cool glass of lemonade."

Nora rose from her chair and went with him to the drink table where he poured them both a cup and put change into a donation jar. Then he guided her to as quiet a spot as they could find and sat on a bench.

"You must come here often," Nora said.

He took a sip of his drink and smiled at her. "Every chance I get," he replied. "I work hard, and this is my form of relaxation."

Nora chuckled. "You work hard at dancing, too."

He nodded. "I guess." His tone changed to be more serious. "What about you, Nora? What are your plans? I know you and Harold are supposed to be a pair. Did you come with me to make him jealous?"

She had to think about it. "I'm not sure."

"That's okay, I don't care if you did. I'm having a great time and I've wanted to ask you out for a long while. Come on, they're playing a slow song that's one of my favorites."

They walked to the dance floor where he pulled her into his strong arms. Nora Brown felt a warm rush of contentment. This man was proving interesting.

If she had consented to come to the dance to push Harold into proposing, how would she respond if he asks her? If she doesn't say yes right away, how is her mother going to respond? Was her usual smooth path getting a little rocky? Nora put these thoughts out of her mind. At the present, she was having the most enjoyable time she'd had in a very long time. The music continued as they moved as one. Whatever tomorrow would bring didn't matter. For tonight, Nora Brown felt secure in the arms of Billy Wood.

Chapter 14

Lockwood had been a flurry of quiet activity and I was tired. Today Dr. Hawthorne was due to return. Peg and I had managed to follow his orders of feeding the babies, but I still held concerns about the tiny Anna. She didn't seem to be thriving as baby Alex was.

As for Miss Adelaide, there was little improvement in her mood, but at least her crying bouts were over. I knew Mr. Alex was concerned about his previously vibrant wife. He came into the room a couple times a day to see the babies and attempt to comfort her. He seemed at a loss of what to do. Peg and I felt the same way. We tried to heed Dr. Hawthorne's words to keep everything as it was before the babies came, but it was not easy to act cheerful as though all was hunky-dory. Visitors had stayed away as Dr. Hawthorne wanted. However, the week had passed and I felt seeing some familiar faces besides mine, Peg's and Mr. Alex's would help improve Miss Addie's outlook. I decided to take it upon herself to ask Miss Lottie and Miss Fannie to come to the big house for tea where it could be served on the front porch.

This sounded like a good plan, but how could I get Miss Adelaide to agree? Then an idea popped into my mind. Why not have Dr. Hawthorne suggest it? Miss Addie put a lot of stock into what Dr. Hawthorne said. Yes, I decided she would have a private conversation with the doctor when he came. Then the thought struck that I might be overstepping my role in the house. It would be better to talk with Miss Peg and she could propose the idea to Dr. Hawthorne.

And that's exactly what I did. Peg was pleased with the plan, and, I guessed, also pleased that she would be the one to present the idea to the doctor when he arrived. Peg liked to be the one in charge.

After he arrived around noon, Peg pulled him aside before he went in to see his patient and the babies.

"What changes have you seen since the last time I was here?" the doctor asked.

"The feeding schedule is working well," said Peg. "Vallie takes care of the nights and we both help during the day. Miss Addie could eat more. She doesn't seem to have much of an appetite."

"How about the crying jags?" he asked.

Peg looked over at me as though I was the one to answer. I could and I did. "I haven't seen another like the last time you came. She is sad at times and will dab her eyes with a handkerchief."

The doctor considered, then nodded. "It seems the medicine in the tea is helping. That's good."

"What about the babies? Are they nursing and taking the goat's milk well?" He took a notebook out of his shirt pocket and scribbled down some notes.

"I think so," said Peg.

I had to speak up. "I don't think little Anna is doing well."

Dr. Hawthorne looked up from the notes he was writing. "Why is that?"

"Baby Alex is developing a strong cry and feels heavier. His color is also better than Anna's."

Dr. Hawthorne sat quietly and tapped his pencil on his lips. After a moment, he put the notebook back in his pocket. "I guess I'd better go in and see what's going on."

Peg and I followed him into where Miss Adelaide and the babies were napping.

Dr. Hawthorne was not one to be a reticent bystander. The first thing he did was walk to the window and open the shutters, "You need to get some sun in here, Adelaide."

"You'll disturb the babies," she said in a flat voice.

"They're not going to wake up unless they're hungry or have a tummy ache," he replied.

"How are you doing? Any pain? Any concerns?" he asked.

Addie shook her head.

"How about nursing? Do the babies seem to be latching on all right?"

I stood by the cradle in case the babies did wake up. Alex moved a little. Anna lay there like a tiny blob in her double blankets.

Dr. Hawthorne examined Adelaide and pronounced she was doing well. Then he came to

77

the babies. He picked up Alex and carried him to the bed where he unwrapped the blanket, checked him all over and wrapped him up again. Alex squirmed but didn't wake.

Then Dr. Hawthorne did the same with Anna. He pulled a straight chair next to Miss Addie and sat for a moment before he spoke.

The room was deadly quiet. I was almost afraid to breathe. Peg stood near the door.

"I'll be honest with you Adelaide, your little boy seems to be doing fine, but your little girl is not thriving."

It was the first time I'd seen Miss Addie showing emotion regarding the welfare of her babies.

Her eyes opened wide. "How can that be? What's wrong with her?" her voice was beginning to rise.

"Babies are very sensitive to their mother's feelings. I think Anna's problems are because this pregnancy has been difficult for you. It's a whole new way of life, a big responsibility you haven't had to face. You aren't the only woman who has dropped to the doldrums after a baby is born and you won't be the last. You have good help and you have good friends right here on the farm. Peg has offered to have an afternoon tea for you, Lottie Bell and Fannie. Are you up to it?"

After a moment she answered, "If you think it will help. I don't like feeling like this."

Dr. Hawthorne put his hand on her arm. "I know you don't and it isn't your fault. Our bodies like to play tricks. In your case it's a natural reaction that you have to work harder to climb out of. I can't give you a magic potion."

He smiled at her as he lifted his hand from her arm. "Get with your friends. I'm sure they're chafing at the bit to see those two beautiful little ones."

I saw a faint smile appear on Miss Addie's face. "I'm sure they are. I just haven't been up to seeing anyone."

Dr. Hawthorne rose from his chair. "You're a strong woman. Give your friends a chance to help you through this tough phase."

Adelaide nodded. "I'll try," she said.

Peg and I followed Dr. Hawthorne out of the room. In the kitchen, he said, "I do see Mrs. Lockwood improving, but not as good as I had hoped. As far as baby Anna is concerned, you can give her sugar water between feedings, and it isn't going to spoil her or be unfair to baby Alex if you hold her a lot. She needs that closeness and feeling of security. That's the best we can do for her."

"What if she doesn't start to pick up?" asked Peg.

"We will cross that bridge when we come to it," Dr. Hawthorne said. "I'll be back in a week. Call me if you need me or Dr. Burke before then."

We watched as he drove down the lane. Peg held a worried look. "I don't know what will happen if something goes wrong with either of the babies."

I didn't answer.

She shook her head. This used to be such a happy house," she murmured.

Chapter 15

Nora woke up early on Sunday morning, it was like any Sunday morning in the Brown house, although today she had a different feeling. Not only did her feet hurt a little after all the dancing of the night before, she wondered if her mother was going to act cool toward her. She had gone against her mother's wishes. And what about Harold? How was he going to treat her?

Nora wished Vallie was here. Vallie may be younger, but she seemed to be more in tune to people or did she just not care what people thought? That was a trait Nora admired about her sister, Vallie did her own thing when she could. Then she wondered how things were going at Lockwood. There hadn't been any word since Luke and Mark returned from driving Vallie to care for Mrs. Lockwood. They brought the word of twins being born but that was all the news they brought.

Nora hurried into her work dress to help get breakfast ready before they went to Stone's Chapel for services. Her mother had told her that it would be an easy meal because Nora would have to see that Lucy and Davey were fed and dressed.

George Sugg was still at the house, which meant he would also need to be fed. He was getting around quite well and Nora thought it was time for him to return home. However, her mother said he needed one more week under her care. The thought went through her mind that her mother may want to bring him to church. If he did come, he had better not sit in Vallie's seat. She shook her head at the thought. No, Mother would not allow that.

After the hub-bub of breakfast, Nora hurried upstairs to put on her Sunday dress. Harold would be arriving soon, or would he? It didn't matter because she was required to go to church.

Harold did arrive in the buggy. Nora was waiting at the door. "Good morning, Harold."

He tipped his hat. "Good morning, Nora."

They walked to the carriage where he offered his hand to her to step up. He climbed into the driver's seat and tapped the reins. It was then he asked, "How was the dance?"

She felt her face flush a deep pink. "It was fine."

"I don't like to dance, you know that," he said, keeping his eyes on the road ahead.

"Yes, I know that. That's why I went when I was invited. I knew some of the dances."

"It would have been better if you had gone with a group," he said.

Nora didn't like the way he said it. "A group didn't ask me. Billy Wood did."

"The understanding is that you are my girl. Billy Wood had no right to ask you. And, you should have refused to go."

"So that I could have sat home, while you went to a cock fight or played poker or whatever

81

you did last night that was so important?" She was beginning to feel hot under the collar. That was no way to feel when going to church.

"I had business to take care of and the man I talked to could only meet last evening." Harold was calm and matter-of-fact. Harold was always calm and matter-of-fact. "I suggest that if Billy Wood or any other man invites you to go dancing, that you refuse."

That did it. "Harold, I've put my life on hold for you for four years. There is no ring on my finger that says I belong to you."

He turned the horse into the parking area at Stone's Chapel. "We both know that I am working at getting my own place before we can formalize our plans." He looked over at her. "This is the first disagreement we've had, and I trust it will be the last. You know I care for you, Nora."

Nora felt a pang of guilt. He was right. "I'm sorry," she said.

They went into the chapel like they always did, and sat in the pew as they always had. Nora's family came in with George Sugg, but he was placed between Mr. Brown and Luke. It had been an uncomfortable morning and Nora felt disgruntled. Where was Vallie when she needed her?

After the service, Harold took her home. When they arrived, he walked her to the door. "I believe we've aired our differences today and we can continue as we always have," he said.

Nora nodded. "It seems that way," she replied. "When will I see you again?"

"I'll drop by on Wednesday. I have to make a trip into Berryville."

Nora smiled. "I could go with you."

He shook his head. "Sorry, I have business to attend to, but I can stop by around dinner time. We can play gin rummy." He kissed her cheek. "I'll see you on Wednesday."

Nora watched him go with mixed feelings. She hadn't felt the pleasant rush she'd felt when Billy Wood brushed a quick kiss on her cheek. She had seen him come into church this morning and he had given her his shy smile.

Nora turned and walked into the kitchen before she went upstairs to change her dress. She poured herself a cup of coffee and sat in the quiet of the house trying to sort out her thoughts before the rest of the family arrived home.

One thing she knew for sure, she needed to talk with Vallie.

Chapter 16

The sandwiches were made, the cookies baked, and the water was ready for tea. Lottie Bell Dunn and Fannie Edwards appeared at the back door of Lockwood together. Lottie was pleasingly plump and Fannie shaped like a turnip with the baby soon to be born. They held smiles a mile wide when Peg opened the door.

"Come right in, ladies," she said. "We're so happy you're here. I have the front porch set up for tea, and as soon as Miss Adelaide and Vallie finish feeding the babies, tea will be served. Come ahead," she motioned and led them to the front porch.

"We're as excited as two kids waiting for Santa Claus," said Fannie.

Lottie nodded her head in agreement. "It's been hard for us to stay away."

"That was Dr. Hawthorne's order," said Peg.

Lottie and Fannie took their seats at the table set with a white cloth, linen napkins and a rose in a short vase in the middle.

In a confidential voice, Lottie said, "Alex is very worried about Addie. How is she doing?"

Peg shook her head. "We're hoping you two friends can brighten her spirits. This has been a difficult time for her. Physically she is doing well but she has been in a sad state since the babies came. I'll go tell them you're waiting."

It was a lovely day with a slight breeze. They sat looking at the Blue Ridge Mountains in the distance.

"I know how she feels," Lottie said. "I was very down after Eddie came. It wasn't the same when Cal and Lizzie were born. I was happy as a lark."

"I hope that's the way I'll feel," said Fannie. "This having babies isn't easy."

Lottie smiled. "No, but it is very rewarding."

They turned when they heard the door open. There stood Adelaide in a white lace robe looking as attractive as ever, but with a false smile on her face.

Lottie rose from her chair and rushed to give Addie a big hug. "We have missed you, dear friend, and we can't wait to feast our eyes on your babies."

"I'd get out of the chair," Fannie said, "but I move like a snail."

"A big one," said Adelaide, and she held an actual smile. She walked to where Fannie sat and gave her a hug before she took her seat at the table. "Vallie is dressing the twins and will bring them out." Addie looked around. "This is the first I have been out of my room in almost two weeks. The sun feels good."

Peg arrived with a tray carrying the sandwiches, cookies, pot of tea and cream and sugar in small containers. "Here you are, ladies. Miss Lottie, I made your favorite cookies."

"Of course you did," said Fannie. "What special did you make for me?"

Peg chuckled. "I put green icing on the sugar cookies. I wasn't sure if there was a special Irish cookie."

Fannie laughed aloud. "If there is, I've never had one."

Peg poured the tea and went back into the house.

"I am glad you're here," Adelaide said. "I'm not very good company."

Lottie took a sip of tea. "Addie do you remember when I was so down? You took me to the river. We had a picnic and went fishing."

Addie nodded. "I remember. You helped me get back into the world. We want to help you get back to the Addie we love."

Addie shook her head. "I don't know if I'll ever feel the same."

"Certainly you will," Fannie said. "We're all a little older, but our personalities don't change. You'll work through this one day at a time."

Addie sipped her tea. "You sound like the doctor."

"I would have been," said Fannie, "but they wouldn't let red-haired women into the medical school."

"That's probably because you sat on the doorstep and refused to move," Lottie quipped.

"How did you know?" Fannie laughed. "The ride in the police paddy wagon was kind of fun."

Adelaide smiled. "You never rode in a paddy wagon."

Fannie shrugged. "No, but I'll bet it would be fun."

The door opened wide and I pushed the wicker carriage holding the twins onto the porch. They were dressed in long white gowns with white sweaters and bonnets to match. A delicate white carriage robe covered them both.

Lottie rose from her chair. She pulled back the carriage robe to get a full view of the babies she had been so anxious to see. "Oh, Addie. They are beautiful. May I hold one of them?"

Addie nodded. Lottie picked up Alex and held him close.

"Do you want to hold Anna?" I asked Fannie.

"I can hardly wait to get my hands on her," Fannie confessed.

I took the little bundle and Fannie had tears in her eyes as she clutched the baby to her chest. "Oh, Addie. She is light as a feather and a joy to hold. I hope in a couple of weeks that we can hold our babies together."

Lottie looked over at her. "That includes me. Addie can only handle one baby at a time. I'll get all the pleasure without the pain."

As I stood waiting, I could tell this was what Miss Adelaide needed, the warmth of the sun and the warmth of her friends would put her on the path of recovery.

I took the babies back to their room because it would be feeding time again.

The ladies finished their tea. Adelaide thanked them for coming.

Lottie said, "I think we should get together on Sunday afternoon for dinner. Our husbands can join us, Caleb and Jess want to see the babies, too."

"I can bake a chicken and a couple loaves of bread," Fannie offered.

"That's good. I'll fix the potatoes and I've got a couple of quarts of green beans I need to use up," said Lottie.

Peg came out to clean up the table and had overheard their conversation. "I'll bake a couple of apple pies for you. Jess likes his apple pie."

"Peg, that would be perfect," said Fannie.

"What do you think, Addie?" Lottie asked.

"I think that would be good for Alex," she said. "I certainly haven't done anything to cheer him up."

Lottie and Fannie left and it was time to feed the babies.

I helped Miss Addie get ready to nurse Alex before she got the bottle of goat's milk to feed Anna. Even if Miss Adelaide was still in a somber mood, there was a lighter feeling to the atmosphere in the room.

Chapter 17

On Sunday afternoon, Peg went to Lottie's house to watch her children while the six friends gathered for dinner. Lottie decided to act as hostess. "Adelaide, you're not ready and Fannie, you deserve to sit. Peg has it all arranged so it is only a matter of serving. Caleb can fill the water glasses and Jess can pour coffee when it's time for dessert."

"What about me?" asked Alex. "Shouldn't I be doing something?"

"You're furnishing the house," said Jess.

The babies were asleep. I heard the good-natured bantering going on in the dining room, and I went out the kitchen door to see Ches. I hadn't had a chance to spend any time with him. It was up to the farm hands to keep him fed and watered. I knew I had a couple of hours to myself for the first time since I had come. I wasn't sure how long Miss Adelaide would need me, but what I thought would only be a couple of weeks was now in the third.

I told Miss Lottie where I would be when I passed her in the kitchen. "You go ahead, Vallie. I know you haven't had any time for yourself. I'll send Caleb if we need you."

Ches was in the corral. I wanted to put a saddle on him and take a long ride, but that would take me too far away from the house. I put the bridle on him and walked him around to give us both some exercise.

"I don't know Ches, this isn't turning out the way I thought it would. We should both be at home. I'm getting a little homesick. How about you?" I patted his neck and he shook his head. I took a lump of sugar from my pocket and he nuzzled my hand as he ate it. I was walking him down the lane when I saw a buggy coming. I knew it was ours, but I couldn't see who was driving it until it got closer.

"Nora! What are you doing here?"

Nora stopped the buggy as I approached.

"I have to talk to you, Vallie. Do you have time?"

"I have about an hour. Let's take the buggy up near the barn, there's a bench we can sit on."

I climbed up next to her and let Ches walk beside the buggy while I held his reins.

"Is everything all right at home?" I knew there had to be a reason she would come by herself.

She nodded. When we got to the bench, I put Ches back into the corral and Nora tied her horse to a tree. The bench was shaded by a big oak tree and held a feeling of privacy. We sat down.

"It's me, Vallie. I'm so mixed up."

"About what?"

"About my relationship with Harold. I went to the barn dance with Billy Wood."

"Good for you," I said.

"Mother wasn't happy."

I laughed. "Knowing Mother, I wouldn't expect she would be. She likes Harold because he's a schmoozer and has a gift of gab."

"But, that's not all." Nora's face held a worried look. "Billy came to the farm last Thursday to take some hogs to the slaughter house for Father. I was out hanging clothes on the clothes line. I waved at him on his way out and he stopped the truck." She hesitated.

"Go on," I urged. "I'm all ears."

"Well, I went over to the truck to talk to him. He said we needed to go dancing again."

"And…?"

"And, I told him I'd like to and that Harold said it was okay if I went with a group."

I shook my head. "What right does Harold have telling you what to do? If you want to go dancing with Billy Wood, go ahead. Nora you need to get rid of Harold."

"That's about what Billy said. Not only that, he said he was thirty, he had his own place, and that it was time he was married and started a family."

"Wow! I can't believe Billy Wood said all that."

Nora Nodded. "He did. Then he said he couldn't wait for me forever."

I felt my eyes open wide. "Holy cow! What did you say?"

"I didn't know what to say, so I laughed and said he couldn't be serious."

"You probably cut him to the quick."

She shrugged. "I don't know. He hopped into the truck, looked out the window and said, 'Think about it Nora.' Then he drove off."

"Did you tell Mother?"

She shook her head. "How can I tell Mother? She saw me walk over to the truck to talk to him and made me feel like a wanton woman. I had to come to talk to you, Vallie. I don't know what I should do."

"Don't be so hard on yourself. If you like Billy, give him a chance. You're the one who has to make the decision."

Nora thought for a minute. "I like Billy a lot; he makes me feel carefree and happy. He is so different than Harold. What if I do stop seeing Harold and Billy changes his mind about me?"

Nora could be exasperating. "Look, Billy isn't going to stick his neck out about such an important matter. He's liked you for a long time, and you didn't pay any attention because Harold got in the way. You need to have some happiness in your life and you're not going to have it with the man who's a selfish freeloader. Open your eyes, Nora."

She gave a deep sigh.

"When are you going to see Billy again?"

"I guess maybe next Sunday in church."

"That's perfect. If I know Harold he'll make it over once during the week at dinner time. You can break it off then."

Nora sat fingering the fringe on a bag she carried, "Vallie, you make everything sound so simple. You don't have a boyfriend."

"No," I said. "If I did it wouldn't be some-body like Harold."

Nora squirmed in her seat. "I don't know if I'm brave enough."

"If you like Billy Wood, you're going to have to be brave enough."

I hoped I had given Nora the encouragement she needed without sounding too harsh. My dear sister needed to be on a different path than the one she was on with Harold.

Nora hugged me before she got in the buggy to start her way home. "I'm so glad I came to talk with you, Vallie. How much longer are you going to be here?"

"I don't know. I guess once Miss Adelaide feels better and the twins are both doing well. I miss being home, Nora."

Nora nodded. "We all miss you. Luke is going to take George Sugg back to the Sugg place this week."

"What about Miss Tizzie?"

"She's still up at the hospital," Nora an-swered.

That caused me to wonder. It seemed a long time to recover from food poisoning. I knew Mother had changed her mind about putting George Sugg in the room we'd fixed up, and a spot was prepared for him on the back porch. Was it in the back of Mother's mind that she would also be caring for Miss Tizzie?

I waved to Nora and watched her drive down the lane. I stopped myself to ask if Ash Corbin was still coming to church. As I watched her ride away, I wished I could have gone with her, but it was time to go to the big house and check on the babies. The precious time for myself was over.

Chapter 18

The twins were three weeks old and it was the week of my nineteenth birthday. Miss Adelaide was beginning to show more interest in her surroundings. This morning she wanted to put on a housedress, stockings and shoes. She sat in front of the mirror and brushed her hair. Until now she had stayed in her nightclothes and robe, and I had been the one to be sure she was groomed.

Mr. Alex came into the room before he went to take care of things in the office. Miss Adelaide had just finished at the dressing table. She turned when he came in and rose from her chair.

He smiled at her. "You're in a dress," he said.

"I thought it was time," she replied, walked over to him and put her arm around his waist. "Have you had breakfast?" she asked.

I stayed in the corner of the room folding diapers. I could see Mr. Alex was a bit confused. "How are you feeling?"

"Better," she said. "I thought that if you haven't eaten, we could have breakfast together."

"We haven't done that for a long time, it seems. I'll talk to Peg. She can set us up in the dining room."

Addie shook her head. "No. Let's go sit on the porch and enjoy the morning sun."

Had it been the reuniting with her friends or the fact that her body was beginning to heal that caused this change? Or was she trying hard to give a sense of normalcy? She told Dr. Hawthorne she was going to try.

Miss Lottie had made a point of coming in every day to have tea, talk with Miss Addie and hold the babies. She said Miss Fannie was due to have her baby any time. If Miss Addie was truly improving and all went well with the birth of a new baby, Lockwood farm might get back to the comfortable place it used to be.

"We shall have coffee on the porch," Mr. Alex said and left the room to have Peg take care of breakfast.

Miss Addie came over to me. "Did I sound believable?"

My heart sunk. Was she putting on an act? "Miss Adelaide, don't give us false hope."

She looked at me with a weak smile. "That's what I like about you, Vallie. You're honest and wise beyond your years."

"Miss Adelaide, why don't you take Anna out on the porch with you? She needs the warmth of the sun and the warmth of her mother." That was a bold statement and I expected a reprimand, but I felt it needed to be said.

She stared at me. "If I can start to like myself, I can start to love my babies."

96

I thought she was going to cry, but she swallowed hard, picked up the sweet Anna, and went to join her husband on the porch.

I finished folding the diapers and straightening up the room. I checked baby Alex who was sound asleep. That's what babies are, I thought: eat, sleep and change diapers. Luckily, neither one of them was a colicky baby. It was difficult enough to put up with the moody Adelaide. I wondered how long she was going to need my help.

Mr. Alex had hired a younger woman to help with the cleaning of the house. That left both Peg and me with more free time. I went to my room, took my colored pencils and drawing paper out of the desk drawer. I was going to turn nineteen in a few days and sketching my ideas of clothing was a way to soothe my mind because, to be honest with myself, I didn't know where my life was headed.

I hadn't sketched as much as I wanted when I heard baby Alex cry. I left the drawings on the desk and went into where he lay in the long cradle. He was still bald as a baseball, but he could smile and his cute little face was getting rounder. I was changing his diaper when Miss Addie and Mr. Alex came into the room. Breakfast must have gone well because Mr. Alex looked contented as did Miss Adelaide.

"I'll hold him while you get his bottle," he said to me. This was a surprise. All Mr. Alex had done up to this point was look at the babies in the cradle and pat the blankets that held them.

I wrapped the baby up in his blanket and handed him to his father before I left to get the bottle of goat's milk. On my trip to the kitchen, all I could think was that the usual routine had taken a big change, and that was fine with me as long as it continued.

I took the bottle of milk from the ice box and heated it in a pan of warm water that Peg always kept on the stove. When I returned to the room, I found Miss Addie changing Anna's diaper. "I can do that," I said.

Miss Addie shook her head. "It's something I need and want to do."

Mr. Alex handed baby Alex to me. "You have been a big help to us, Vallie." He kissed the baby's forehead and handed him to me before he went to his wife. "Do you need me for anything?" he asked her.

She offered a genuine smile. "No. Thank you for asking. I know you have a busy day ahead of you."

He kissed her cheek and left the room.

Miss Adelaide sat in the rocking chair to nurse baby Anna. This was the closeness between mother and child I had wished to have seen when they were born. I had something good to report to Dr. Hawthorne who was to visit in a couple of days. I did believe that Miss Adelaide was beginning to climb out of her despair, and I was sure Dr. Hawthorne would see that for himself.

This new day had started out better than any day I had spent at Lockwood. I could only hope that it would continue, so that I could return to the comfort of my family and the familiar way of life on our farm.

Chapter 19

Wednesday was my birthday. I hadn't told anyone in the house for the fact that I didn't think it would matter to them. Would anyone at Lockwood care if I was eighteen or nineteen?

It would have stayed that way except Nora came over in the buggy right after lunchtime. That was fortunate because we had finished feeding the babies and they and Miss Adelaide were napping.

I had taken the empty baby bottle to the kitchen, and I saw the buggy coming up the lane.

"I wonder who that is," said Miss Peg.

"It's my sister," I said. "I hope everything is all right at the farm."

"You go ahead on out there and talk to her. I'll take care of the bottle," Miss Peg said as she continued working around in the kitchen.

Nora stopped the buggy when I came off the back porch to meet her.

I didn't even say hello. I said, "Is everything all right at home?"

Nora smiled, "Happy Birthday, Vallie. Everything is fine at home."

I don't know what I expected to hear, but I let out a sigh of relief. "I didn't think anyone remembered."

"Mother has sent a package. Where do you want me to put the horse and buggy?"

I climbed up beside her. "Let's go out by the barn where we were before. I want to know what you've decided about Harold."

She drove the buggy, hitched the horse to a tree and asked, "Have you got some time?"

"Time enough to hear what you have to say." The fact that I had a birthday box waiting didn't even enter my mind. We sat together on the bench.

Nora looked at me. "Harold came by the house last Wednesday. After dinner we sat on the porch. I told him I was mixed up about my feelings."

"What did he say?"

"He said, 'Feelings about what?' which I figured he might guess as we had that tiff the Sunday before."

Nora continued, "I said, about my feelings for you and for Billy Wood."

"Did that rile him?"

"He laughed." Nora shrugged her shoulder. "It bothered me that he didn't think I was serious. So in the next breath I heard myself say I didn't want to see him anymore."

I looked at her. "How did he take it?"

"He said I'd get over it and he would pick me up on Sunday for church."

I shook my head. "That sounds like him."

Nora put her hand on my arm. "That made me question myself. Then I thought of you, Vallie. You told me I would have to be brave. I got up from my seat on the porch and told him he could come by, but I wouldn't go with him."

Nora sat for a moment. "Vallie, he didn't say a word. He just got up and left. It was like he didn't care."

"Did he come by on Sunday?"

Nora took her hand from my arm and pulled out her handkerchief to dab at her eyes. "After four long years, I found out that I was a convenience. I went to church with the family. Harold didn't show up. People asked me if he was sick."

I chuckled. "So you told them that you didn't know and that you and Harold had broken up."

Then Nora smiled. "In so many words. I hoped the news would get to Billy."

I laughed. "There's no way he's not going to hear it. That has got to be the big news on the gossip line."

"Mother isn't too pleased about it. I know she wants to see me married. She did say that if I was sure about my decision, it may be the right choice."

"Nora, you've brought me the best birthday present I could have hoped for."

Nora rose from the bench. "I couldn't keep it to myself and bringing your present was the perfect way to get to see you."

I got up to stand beside her. "I can hardly wait to see what Mother has packed up, but I don't have time to open it now. I'll take it to my room." I hugged Nora. "Thanks for coming. I hope it isn't too much longer that I am needed here."

"We can use you at home. Mother has brought Tizzie Nelson to the house. Vallie, poor

Tizzie is skin and bones. I don't think she's going to last too much longer."

My face fell. "That is sad. Tizzie has been good to me."

Nora took the present from the back of the buggy and handed it to me before she took her place at the reins.

"Tell Mother thank you, and that I miss being home." I said.

"Of course I will." Nora tapped the reins and quickly pulled up on them, "I almost forgot. Luke said to tell you that Vern Corbin's nephew asked about you after church on Sunday." Then she chuckled, started the horse, and called over her shoulder, "Happy Birthday, Vallie."

Nora drove off down the lane leaving me to think about Ashton Corbin. I had been so involved in my position here at Lockwood that he had slipped my mind. I liked thinking about him and I liked that he had asked about me. Could my birthday be any better?

I carried my wrapped box to the big house. If Peg wasn't in the kitchen, I could sneak it to my room without any questions.

I was in luck.

That evening when I was alone I opened the box Mother had sent. In it was a pale yellow blouse she had made with embroidery on the collar, and a tan skirt with shiny brown buttons trimming one side. It would be perfect to wear to a dance, I thought and smiled to myself. My chance at going dancing was as likely as my going to see the Eiffel Tower.

Mother also sent my favorite molasses cookies and a tin of fudge she had made. I knew Mother had put a lot of time and love into my nineteenth birthday. That gladdened my heart and increased my desire to return home.

Chapter 20

The next week brought the good news that Jess and Fannie Edwards were the parents of a baby boy. It happened one afternoon when Jess was out in the field. Fannie had time to ring the bell that summoned help, but by the time Lottie got to the cabin, the baby was already there.

I heard the conversation when Miss Lottie came to tell Adelaide about it. They were having coffee in Addie's room, each holding one of the babies. I was changing the linens on the bed.

"It just happened so fast," Miss Lottie said. "By the time I walked in the door all I had to do was make sure the baby was breathing and cut the cord."

"Was Fannie all right?" asked Adelaide.

"She was fine. She lay on the bed as though this was an everyday occurrence and said, 'I don't believe in long labors.' I came in the cabin shaky as a leaf not knowing what I was going to find. Fannie made me laugh and all that anxiety flew away. Wait until you see him, Addie. He's going to be big like Jess."

Miss Addie laughed aloud. Her laugh was like music to my ears. It had been over a month since I had come and watched as she transformed from a depressive state to the strong Miss Addie I knew.

She wasn't completely back, but it wouldn't be long. Perhaps Dr. Hawthorne was correct in that birthing babies causes changes to the body. Something about hormones. Whatever the cause, I was glad that the sadness had passed.

The twins were doing well. Alex gained as he should and Anna was beginning to catch up. Her color was good and her cry almost as strong as her brother's. That caused me to wonder if baby girls were more in tune to a mother's feelings than baby boys. Maybe sensing moods was a more astute trait. Maybe that was the difference between men and women. Maybe I was overloading my brain, so I finished making the bed and left the two ladies talking.

Miss Lottie had been a big help. She and Miss Adelaide had been friends since they were young, growing up in tenant houses on a big estate. Their lives had taken different paths, but they were still close friends. Once when Miss Lottie came by, I was sitting on the back porch doing some sketching. She had looked at my designs and said I should take them to Irene Butler and see if she was interested in using them for her dress shop.

That thought hadn't occurred to me as sketching designs of clothing was something I did for fun. What if Irene Butler wanted to buy them? The thought was fleeting. Everyone knew Irene Butler pinched her pennies. According to what I had heard, Miss Lottie was a very good seamstress also, and had once worked in the Butler dress shop. As I thought about it, I remembered hearing she and

Miss Addie talk about their trip to Colorado, how she had made a taffeta dress for Miss Addie to wear to a concert, and that a man Miss Lottie worked for gave her an expensive sewing machine.

However, today wasn't free time to get out my sketch book, but there was enough time to go to the corral and check on my horse.

Even though Ches was let out for exercise every day, I knew he was as antsy to get back to our farm as I was.

I walked into the corral, put the bridle on and led him outside of the penned in area. "It won't be too much longer," I said to him."There is much improvement in the big house. Maybe I can get enough time that we can go on a long ride. Wouldn't that be good for both of us?" I patted his neck and gave him a piece of carrot I had brought in my pocket. "I don't know, Ches. I've had to do a lot of thinking since I've been here. I'm nineteen and I don't know where my life is going. All Nora wants to do is get married, keep a house, and have a family. That's not what I want. You know, Ches, I don't know what I want." He nudged my shoulder. "I don't have another carrot," I told him. We had walked around the yard near the barn and it was time for me to go back in the house. I put him in the corral, took off the bridle and pulled a lump of sugar from my pocket. Then I hugged his neck before I left for the house in a melancholy mood.

My expression must have given me away because when I walked into the kitchen Miss Peg said, "What's the matter with you?"

"Nothing's the matter," I replied.

"You know what I think," Miss Peg said. "I think you need to make a visit to your home."

I shrugged. "What makes you think that?"

"I saw that wistful look in your eye when your sister left last week. I know Mr. Alex has been interviewing nannies."

"Nannies?" The only nannies I knew were goats.

"Yes. It's an educated woman to come and take care of the babies, so that Miss Adelaide can get back to doing the bookwork for this place. Mr. Alex has been trying to do her job and his since the babies came."

"Why didn't he hire a bookkeeper?" I asked, as though that made sense to me.

"Miss Addie didn't want anyone to touch the books but herself and Mr. Alex. The sooner she can get back to what she likes to do, the sooner this house can get back to the way it used to be."

"It will never be the same with the two babies in it." Didn't I act like the wise one?

Peg didn't reply.

"When do you think the nanny will come?" I said. "Do you think I can go back to helping clean the house a couple times a week?"

Peg turned from the stove and smiled at me. "It won't be long, Vallie. Talk with Mr. Alex about work."

And, it wasn't long. Mr. Alex called me into his office on Saturday morning. I still felt timid in his presence. "Vallie, I have a woman coming to take care of the babies on Monday. This will be your last weekend here. We've been through a lot together, and you have been the mainstay through this rough time. I thank you. He handed me an envelope, which I put in my apron pocket.

"Will you still need me a couple times a week like before the babies came?"

He actually smiled at me. "Certainly," he said. "We couldn't do without you."

Coming from Mr. Alex that made me feel a mile high, and I left the room with a rosy glow. I could hardly contain my joy at the thought that I would be going home.

Chapter 21

I didn't tell anyone in my family that I was coming home. Mr. Edwards helped me tie up my bundle of belongings and secured it behind the saddle.

"You travel light, Miss Vallie. Just like a cowboy," he said while he was arranging the pack on Ches.

"Were you a cowboy, Mr. Edwards?"

He nodded. "Yes, I was and so was Caleb. That's how we learned to handle these ornery cattle."

"At home, we call them cows," I said.

"Well, Miss Vallie," he rested his arm on the saddle and looked at me. "There are cows and there are cattle. At your place they give milk so they're cows. The ones here are mostly used for meat so they're called cattle."

That was confusing to me, and I said, "The females have babies so I call them cows, and the males father the offspring so I call them bulls."

He took his arm from the saddle and went back to tying up my things.

"I can't fault you there, but you'd better not let an authentic cowboy hear you say that. They take pride in their cattle."

I shrugged. "I probably won't ever meet a real cowboy. I don't get too far from home."

Mr. Edwards was a big man. He always wore a cowboy hat and cowboy boots. "You're looking at a genuine, dyed-in-the-wool cowboy. But, Miss Vallie, if you want to call these cattle cows, that's all right with me."

I couldn't help but smile. I liked Mr. Edwards, "I promise I won't say it so you can hear."

That made him smile.

"I saw your baby boy yesterday. I think he's going to have Miss Fannie's red hair."

He grinned from ear to ear. "He's a big guy. You'd better come back and see us and watch all these babies grow."

He was through fixing the pack on Ches and he helped me up into the saddle.

"I'll be coming two days a week as I did before the babies came."

"We'll look for you. Don't push Ches on the way home. It wouldn't do for that bundle to topple off."

"I'll be careful," I replied. "Thank you for your help."

"You've got a fine horse. He'll be glad to get back and have the run of the field." He knew I was antsy to be on my way. He slapped my horse on the rump and we were off.

I had been at Lockwood for six weeks. It was the end of July and the day was hot. Although I was eager to get home, I knew I couldn't push Ches into a fast pace. I stopped at the Longmarsh Run so he could get a drink, and I could wet a handkerchief to wash my face and neck. That would refresh both of us until we reached home.

Lucy and Davey saw us first. I heard them shout, "Vallie's home!" Then I saw Mother and Nora coming out of the house, and Father and the boys coming around the corner of the barn. I was finally here. I swallowed hard and fought back the urge to cry. They would be tears of happiness and relief. However, it wouldn't do to have my family see me cry no matter what kind of tears they were. I swung out of the saddle and received a warm welcome from each one.

Father said, "Vallie, if we knew you were coming I would have sent one of the boys to drive you home in the buggy. That's a pretty good packing job atop Ches."

"Mr. Edwards did it for me. I wanted to get home so bad that I didn't want to wait for someone to come and get me."

"We have your favorite dinner of fried chicken," Mother said. "And most of the vegetables in the garden are ripe. We'll have a meal fit for Passover. You must be tired. Come in the house and freshen up. Luke and Mark can put Ches in the pasture and carry in your belongings."

Nora put her arm through mine as we walked to the kitchen door. "We've got some catching up to do," she said.

"I like the sound of that."

When we got in the house, Mother poured tea in a glass. "I need to check on Miss Tizzie."

I had forgotten about Miss Tizzie. I wasn't sure I wanted to see her, at least I knew I didn't want to see her right at this moment.

Mother left the room and Nora whispered, "Tizzie sleeps most of time. She asks about you, Vallie. It's good you've come because I think she's on her way out of this world."

I shook my head. "I know I will have to see her, but I don't want to spoil my gladness at being home. I'll see her tomorrow."

That was fine with Mother. She said, "After dinner, you and Nora can go up to your room. You'll be taking care of Tizzie tomorrow."

My heart sank. Did I just leave six weeks of being a nursemaid to come home to do the same? But, taking care of a young mother and her babies was a whole lot different from taking care of a dying woman.

When Nora and I were getting ready for bed, I asked, "Why do you think Mother has decided I should take care of Tizzie? I don't think that's fair."

Nora was in her summer nightgown. "That's obvious. She believes that will be easier than working around the house. The vegetables are ripe, which means canning and pickling, and next week the tomatoes will start. I'll switch places with you."

I thought about it. "Maybe I should have stayed at Lockwood another month. I forgot all about tomatoes and corn and haying season."

Nora flopped down on her bed. I wish I could forget about it," she turned on her side and propped herself up on one elbow. "I'm going to the cinema with Billy Wood on Saturday. I can think about that while I'm putting up dill pickles."

"Oh, Nora, that's wonderful. I guess Harold is out of the picture for good."

"It would appear that way. He's bringing Frances Kline to church."

I shook my head. "Of course he is. She's homely as a hedge fence and probably thirty years old, but she inherited her parents' place."

Nora lay on her back and looked up at the ceiling. "I was such a fool. Mother liked Harold."

I threw my light cotton gown over my head. "Harold is smooth. Father once said he's a conniver."

"Well, whatever he is, Frances can have him."

I was happy for my sister, and I was happy to be home. I pulled back the sheet and lay in my familiar comfortable bed.

Chapter 22

Nora was right. I knew the minute I saw Tizzie lying on the cot that she was not going to be with us much longer. I was prepared before I walked into the room, still, her appearance was a shock.

I went over to the bed with her breakfast of milk toast and scrambled eggs. She opened her glazed eyes and looked at me. "Girl, where have you been?"

That was the Miss Tizzie I remembered. She always called me, Girl. "I've been taking care of Mrs. Lockwood and her twin babies," I answered.

Her voice was weak, but there was nothing wrong with her mind. "You better go over and check on my place."

"Mother has been sending my sister and brother over to keep an eye on it until you can go home. You need to eat your breakfast."

"Now, don't be telling me what I need. I want you to go to my place. Under my bed is a wood box. Bring it to me."

I propped a big pillow behind to raise her head. "If you'll eat some breakfast first," I said. "Don't let these scrambled eggs get cold."

She took a bite of eggs and two spoons of the warm milk toast. "There, I ate it," she said. "Now go on over and get my box."

114

"Mother said you should drink this tea."

"It won't do no good. Girl, I know I'm dying." This was said in a matter-of-fact weak scratchy voice.

What could I say? I knew it was true. I pulled the pillow from behind her and rested her back down. "I'll go over and get your box and make sure everything is the way you want it."

A satisfied look came over her and she drifted back to sleep.

Mother and Nora were in the kitchen when I brought the tray of breakfast food back. "She only took a couple bites. She wants me to go to her place and get a box for her."

Mother was at the sink and didn't turn. "Then you'd better go and get it. Take Lucy and Davey with you."

That meant I would have to hitch up the buggy, but I knew better than to groan aloud. I said, "I'll be back as soon as I can." Then Mother turned to look at me.

"You don't have to hurry, Vallie May. You know how Miss Tizzie likes her house to look, so you take your time and make sure all is in order."

Vallie May. I detested that name. Perhaps one day I would learn to live with it. That was unlikely.

Lucy and Davey were excited to go for a ride. Lucy brought her doll with her and Davey brought a long stick so he could hit the bushes along the way.

Tizzie's house had a forlorn look to it. It was never a place to admire, but the chickens were

115

gone. They, at least, made it look alive. I wondered what happened to the chickens and wondered if the Suggs had helped themselves to some Sunday dinners.

"Luke and Mark brought the chickens to our house," Lucy said. "Miss Tizzie was worried about them."

I should have thought of that. No, I was quick to make a judgement against the Suggs. Then I felt guilty and promised myself I wouldn't jump to conclusions again. I knew that would be an idle promise.

I went in the house and left the children to explore. The place looked like it always did. I could see Luke and Nora had dusted and swept the floors and the front porch. I went into Miss Tizzie's bedroom, got down on my knees and lifted the side of the bedspread. The wooden box was about two feet long and almost as wide. I dragged it out. There were two rope handles on the sides, which made it less cumbersome to carry.

I checked the other bedroom before I took the box outside and put it in the buggy. Davey was excited about finding a baby toad and Lucy had picked a handful of daises.

"Look, Vallie. Aren't they pretty?" she said, holding them up for me to admire.

"They are indeed. Let's go back in the house and see if there is a vase we can put them in. I think that will make Miss Tizzie happy."

We didn't find a vase, so I put water in a quart jar and placed the flowers in it to keep them from wilting on our trip back home.

"Davey, I think you should leave that toad here because this is where he lives." I wasn't too thrilled about a toad jumping around in the buggy.

"I'll hold onto him." I didn't want to quash his enthusiasm and look like the bad sister, therefore we started home with a quart jar of flowers, a half-grown toad, and the treasured box of Tizzie Nelson.

When we got to the Suggs' place, George Sugg was waiting at the side of the road. I didn't want to stop, but I had to as he was almost standing in the path.

"Hello," I said. He didn't answer.

He walked to Davey and handed him a sling-shot he had made. "Wow, Mr. Sugg. You said you'd make me one."

George Sugg smiled and stepped away from the buggy. I tapped the reins and headed on home with Davey looking back and waving at the simple man who had brought a ray of sunshine to his day.

When we got home Davey jumped out of the buggy and ran to show his older brothers his sling-shot. Mark took it from him, put a pebble in it and sent it sailing into the air.

"Hey, that's mine. I'm going to tell Mother you took it from me," Davey hollered.

"Go ahead," said Mark. "She won't let you have it because she'll be afraid you'll be flinging rocks all over the place."

Davey was doing his best to try to get it out of his brother's hand. "Come on, Mark. Give it back."

"Mark," I hollered from the buggy, "stop teasing and give him the sling-shot."

Mark wrinkled his nose when he looked at me. "Oh, all right. Here take it before you become a crybaby."

Davey grabbed his new toy and shouted as he ran toward the house, "I'm not a crybaby!"

I stood and shook my head. It was good to be home.

Miss Tizzie was asleep when I returned. Mother told me to wake her up so she could have some chicken broth. I doubted Tizzie was going to swallow down the broth, but after I took her box in and set it on a chair, I went back to the kitchen for the broth. Mother had put crackers on a tray along with a small pot of hot tea.

I went back into the room and found Miss Tizzie eyeing the box and very much awake, at least for the condition she was in.

"I see you brought my box, Girl." Her voice croaked like a frog.

"It was right where you said it would be," I said.

"Well, go on and open it."

"Mother says you have to take some broth and tea. She has also sent a couple of crackers. It's time you ate some lunch because you didn't eat much for breakfast. Mother works hard all day." If I was trying to shame her, it wasn't working.

"You go on and open my box, and don't try to bribe me into eating something first."

I looked down at her, nodded my head. "That's exactly what I'm going to do. I'm going to leave that box right where it is until you take some broth and tea."

She clamped her mouth shut, which I ignored and went on propping her with a pillow and putting a towel on her chest to catch any spillage.

Picking up the bowl of broth and a spoon, I waited until she opened her mouth. I could be as stubborn as this old woman.

After a silent minute or two, she slowly opened her mouth and surprised me by taking almost all of it. Was that because she was anxious about her box or was she hungry? She also ate one cracker and took some sips of tea.

The thought struck me this might be the calm before the storm. Once she is satisfied that all is in order regarding the contents, is she going to just pass away? There were times when I found myself overthinking a situation.

After taking the tray back to the kitchen, I placed the box on a small side table that I had pulled next to the bed. Tizzie was still propped up on the pillow so she could see what I was taking from her cherished box.

When I opened it my jaw dropped when I saw the contents. To my young eyes, it looked like junk. Undaunted, I went about the business of holding up each item for Miss Tizzie to review.

First, I held up a worn Bible. "Open the cover," she said.

I did, inside the cracked leather cover in a beautiful script was written, *Given to Garland and Elizabeth Nelson on their wedding day, June 10, 1875.*

"Miss Tizzie!" I exclaimed. "That was fifty years ago."

She offered a weak smile, "Yes, I was fifteen-years-old. The Bible was from my grandmother."

Next was a cloth bag held together with snaps. I unsnapped it to find a white baby bonnet and white baby's christening gown that had yellowed with age. I unfolded it and held it for her to see.

Miss Tizzie's bony hand came up to finger the delicate material. She was silent as if drifting back to remember. "That was my baby's. He only lived four months." It was said with a wistful edge to her voice.

In a velvet pouch was a gold bracelet. The filigreed design made it a beautiful piece of jewelry. "Oh, Miss Tizzie, what a lovely bracelet. Do you want me to put it on your wrist?"

Another weak smile appeared. "That's for you, Vallie. You're like the daughter I never had."

My ears were quick to catch the fact that she hadn't called me, Girl. Then I knew my Miss Tizzie wasn't going to be with us much longer.

This set me back on my heels. "I would love to own it. Isn't there someone in your family you would like to pass it down to?"

She ignored my question. "Put it on," she said. "I want to see it on a young arm like mine used to be."

I felt myself wanting to cry and knew I would if I tried to speak, so I kept silent, put the bracelet on, and held my wrist for her to see. "Miss Tizzie, I have never worn such a pretty piece of jewelry. I will keep it for special times in my life and think of you."

She nodded her head.

Finally, I pulled out a folder of papers which held the deed to her place. There were also a couple of deteriorating pieces of paper I was unable to read. "I'm sorry I can't make out the writing on these papers. Are they letters?"

She actually smiled. "Throw them away. They were love notes from Garland. That deed's important. I want my place to go to somebody who's going to take care of it." Her voice was the strongest at this point than it had been since yesterday.

A thought hit my mind. I had heard Miss Fannie saying that Mr. Edwards wanted to buy his own place. Miss Fannie didn't want to move because she liked the little cabin they lived in at Lockwood. I wondered if Mr. Jess would have any interest in owning Miss Tizzie's place. Her house wasn't much different from the cabin, and I knew Mr. Jess would put great care into making it a working farm.

"Miss Tizzie," I said. "I know somebody who might be interested in your place. They live over on Lockwood and just had a baby. I know he wants his own place, and he would take care of it."

She looked at me with her glazy eyes. "You bring him to me. If I want to die happy."

I had to laugh. "Miss Tizzie, you might just outsmart yourself and live another ten years."

"You go do as I say, Girl." Then she ordered me to take the pillow from behind her back so she could sleep.

I put the summation of Miss Tizzie's life back in the box, closed the lid and sat it on a straight chair. She was asleep before I left the room.

Mother was in the kitchen, as she usually was, preparing the lunchtime meal.

"Mother I went through the box with Miss Tizzie. There wasn't much in it, I have to feel sorry for her. She hasn't had much happiness in her life."

"Tizzie Nelson is a strong woman," Mother said. She turned and looked at me, opened her mouth to speak and saw the bracelet I was wearing. "Vallie, where did you get that bracelet?"

"Miss Tizzie gave it to me. She said I was the daughter she never had." I could tell Mother was mulling it over in her head as to whether I should keep the bracelet or give it back. I blurted out, "She wants to sell her place."

That subject overrode the bracelet. "Maybe Harold will buy it."

I wanted to sink through the floor. Did she still have hopes for Nora to marry Harold? I sometimes found my mother confusing.

I replied, "She wants someone who'll take care of it. I was thinking of the Edwards. Mr. Jess wants his own farm and they just had that new baby."

Mother shook her head. "Tizzie's house isn't much."

"Neither is the cabin they live in, but Miss Fannie loves it and has fixed it up to be very homey."

"I'm still going to work at Lockwood two days a week. I'm going to tell Mr. Edwards." And, I intended to tell him before Harold got wind of it.

Chapter 23

It was my day to go back to work at Lock-wood. I was happy to get out of hanging clothes on the clothesline. I was also happy to saddle Ches. "Just the two of us, Ches, won't that be a pleasant ride? You don't even have to carry any big package like when we came home on Saturday."

I gave him a drink of water from a bucket near the stall. Mother and Nora had crocheted two sacques and bonnets for the Lockwood babies. I thought I should take something for Jess and Fannie's baby, but I didn't know what. I wasn't into that kind of handwork. I told Nora that I wish I could take a present, and that evening she sewed up a gown with some pretty white cotton material she had. She washed it in baking soda and vinegar to make it as soft as the baby's skin. Then she wove light blue ribbon around the neck so it could be tied. Mother found a small flat basket with a lid. She folded the gown as pretty as you please, making me proud to present this gift to Miss Fannie.

When we reached Lockwood, Ches walked right into the corral. He had spent enough time in there it must have felt almost like home. After I removed the saddle, blanket and bridle, I gave him a handful of corn I'd carried in a paper bag in my pocket. The farm was quiet except for the sound of a tractor in a nearby field. I liked the quiet of the country.

Peg was waiting for me and opened the back door when I walked onto the porch. "It's good you're here, Vallie. These babies have added a lot of work."

"Where's the nanny?" I asked.

"She says that she is hired to care for the babies, which doesn't include the work of a maid." I could tell by the tone of her voice that she was not too pleased with the new employee. "I'm going to have to talk to Mr. Alex because it is too much for me to handle."

"Miss Peg, I'll still be coming two days a week."

"I know, but I could use you five days a week."

I hoped she wasn't going to ask Mr. Alex about me coming five days a week. I didn't like the sound of that. Although Miss Tizzie wasn't going to be alive too much longer, I didn't want to tie up my week. There was plenty I could do at home, and I did have that one hundred dollars Mr. Alex paid me for the six weeks I was here. On the few occasions I had the chance to spend money, I could do very well on my two dollars a week from working two days a week at Lockwood.

I took a broom, dustpan and dust cloth from the pantry. "Do you want me to start upstairs?" I asked Peg.

"I guess," answered Peg. "The other girl Mr. Alex had hired quit the day after the nanny arrived."

"Miss Adelaide has moved back upstairs. The babies are in the nursery and Miss Gilbert is in the room across from them. I'd like it if you cleaned out the room you stayed in and the one Miss Addie used for her bedroom. Get this place back in some kind of order."

"All right," I agreed. I hadn't heard Miss Peg sound as disgruntled as she was today. I was glad to leave her in the kitchen.

My day passed quickly. I spent a good deal of time cleaning the downstairs rooms. When I finished with them I had Peg check them all over to see if there was anything I missed. One thing was for sure, they smelled a lot better than when I started. I don't think they had been touched after I left five days ago.

I met Miss Gilbert when I went upstairs to clean. She was plain looking, mid-thirties, with a sour expression. I introduced myself. She nodded as she left the room for me to clean.

Miss Adelaide, on the other hand, seemed overjoyed to see me. "Vallie, come right in. I'm pleased you're here. Have you seen the babies, yet?"

"Hello, Miss Addie. I haven't had the chance to see them. You look so much better. How do you feel?"

She rushed over to me and took my hand. "I am back in the world. It's different, but I'm looking on the bright side. I'm sorry it was such a glum time when you were here. Leave your broom and dustpan and come with me. You have to see my babies."

It was good to hear her upbeat. I wondered if it was the addition of Miss Gilbert. From my first impression of the woman, I doubted it. There I was again making a snap judgement. It didn't matter the cause, I liked this Miss Addie.

The nursey was darkened and quiet. Both Alex and Anna were napping when we crept into the room. Miss Addie carefully lifted the blankets from the sleeping pair. They were no longer in the big cradle, they were now in separate cribs.

Alex was still bald and looked like he had grown. Anna's black hair looked silky and shiny and she had a rosy glow. I don't think she had grown, but she looked healthy. We crept out of the room as quietly as we had entered.

In the hall, Miss Addie said, "They are beautiful, aren't they?"

I nodded. "Miss Adelaide, I have a present for Alex and Anna. I left them in the kitchen."

"Don't bother to go and get them. I'll come along with you to get something to eat. I seem to have a ravenous appetite."

In the kitchen, she opened the things Mother and Nora had crocheted. "Oh my, Vallie, such lovely hand work. Did you make them?"

I shook my head. "I'm not good at that sort of thing. I leave that up to my mother and my sister."

Miss Addie laughed. "That's right, you're the one who is the talented sketcher. I know because Lottie told me."

I felt my face blush. "I do that for fun," I said.

"If you impressed Lottie, I know you are good at it. When I get back to my former self perhaps you can design some clothes for me."

I didn't answer. Miss Addie was busy cutting a hunk of cheese from a big cheese wheel. I don't know where Peg had disappeared to, but it was time for me to leave. "I'll be back on Monday. Miss Peg said she can use my help on Mondays and Thursdays."

"Then I'll look for your return. Vallie, thank you for your thoughtful gifts for my little ones, and thank your mother and sister also." She put a slice of cheese between two soda crackers and went toward the office.

In the tote bag I carried, I had the present for Miss Fannie's baby. It was close to five o'clock and I wanted to get on home. I walked to the cabin about a hundred yards away from the big house and knocked on the door. Miss Fannie opened it with the baby in her arms.

"Vallie?" I could tell she was surprised.

"Hello, Miss Fannie, I've brought something for the baby."

"Come on in," she offered.

"No, thank you. I have to get on home." I handed her the gift. "You look very nice." I might have been comparing her to Miss Addie after her babies were born, and Miss Addie didn't look as bright and happy as Miss Fannie did.

"And, here is Daniel J. Edwards," she said and opened the blanket to show me a robust round baby who looked twice the size of baby Alex.

"Gosh, he's almost half grown," I said.

She laughed and snuggled him close. "I'm sorry you can't stay. It was sweet of you to remember us."

I turned to leave, stopped and turned back. "Miss Fannie, I know where there's going to be a farm for sale. Do you mind if I tell Mr. Jess about it?"

She shook her head, "I don't mind. He'll probably hear about it anyway."

"Bye, Miss Fannie."

"Goodbye, Vallie. Thank you for bringing Daniel a present."

I hurried to the corral to saddle up Ches. "Let's go home," I said to him. "I'm tired."

I heard a deep voice say, "Are you talking to your horse?"

Jess Edwards was standing outside the corral. He laughed. "Don't be embarrassed, I talk to my horse all the time."

I knew my face was red, but I put my foot in the stirrup and sat in the saddle as though it wasn't. "Hi, Mr. Edwards. I just saw your baby boy. He's a right nice baby."

"That he is Miss Vallie. Come on out. I'll latch the gate for you."

"Mr. Edwards, I know where there's going to be a farm for sale."

He latched the gate and turned to me. "Where is it?"

"Not far from where I live over on the road to Charles Town. It belongs to Tizzie Nelson. She's staying at our house 'cause she's awful sick. If you're interested she wants to meet you. Can you come tomorrow?"

He cocked his head to one side. "That soon?"

"To be truthful, I don't know how long she's going to last. She wants somebody to buy her place that's going to take care of it. That's why I thought of you."

"That was good thinking," he replied. "I don't see why I can't be there. What time is good?"

"Around lunch time." Didn't I sound like a deal maker?

"I'll do my best to get over there," he said and touched a finger to his cowboy hat to say goodbye.

Chapter 24

Jess arrived at the Brown farm around noon. I had told Miss Tizzie that he was coming, and she seemed satisfied that she might meet a person who would take care of her place after she was gone. She actually ate some oatmeal and drank a small glass of milk for breakfast.

I heard the farm truck as it lumbered down the lane to our house. Father and the boys were out working in the field, Nora and Mother were preparing the lunch meal, and I was finishing cleaning Tizzie's room.

"Miss Tizzie, Mr. Edwards is here. I'm going to prop you up with a pillow so you can talk to him."

"Make me look alive?" she said.

I had to chuckle. "You are alive. You can sit right up there as pretty as a picture."

A weak smile appeared. "Girl, I'm glad you came back," she droned. Miss Tizzie was back to her affectionate way of calling me, Girl.

I heard Mother greet Jess before they appeared at the door of the small room.

"Mr. Edwards is here," Mother announced.

He was a big man and the room seemed to dwarf as he stepped in. "Mrs. Nelson," he said in his deep pleasant tone, "I'm Jess Edwards and I'm pleased to meet you."

The invalid had perked up a bit. "It's Tizzie, and you're a big one."

He smiled at her, "That I am. Miss Vallie told me that you may sell your farm. That's the reason I'm here."

She stared at him with her old eyes. It was a moment before she spoke. "I've got about two hundred acres that I lease out. It's no good to me now."

"I've been looking for property. My wife and I have a new baby, and it's time we had our own place."

"Where's your wife?" Tizzie asked.

"To be honest, she refused to stay home, and she's waiting in the truck. She said she needed to get out for a ride. I thought it was too soon for her and the baby to be out, but my wife has a mind of her own." Then he chuckled, "She wants to see your place before I make a decision without her."

I knew Miss Fannie did not want to leave their cabin at Lockwood, which made me wonder what her reaction would be when we went to the Nelson place.

"I want to see her," Tizzie said.

Jess went out to the farm truck, talked to Fannie, who was holding Daniel in her arms. He helped her out of the seat so she could come in and meet Tizzie.

She entered the room and walked right over to Tizzie with her hand outstretched. "I'm Fannie Edwards," she said, "and this is our baby. He's growing." She unwrapped the blanket for Tizzie to see him.

A wrinkled hand came up to touch the sleeping little one. Tears came to her eyes, and I knew it was a reminder of her baby who had died.

I spoke up. "It's been a long morning. If Miss Tizzie agrees, I can take you over to show you her place."

Tizzie nodded and touched the baby again.

Mother came to the doorway. "We'll have lunch in about an hour," she said to Jess. "We'd like to have you stay and eat with us."

"That's very nice, but…"

Fannie interrupted, "Of course we will."

Tizzie looked at the red-haired, Irish young woman and put her hand on Fannie's arm. "I like you."

Coming from Tizzie Nelson that was a high compliment.

After I settled her tired body back so she could nap, I put on my sun hat, then went out and climbed in the back of the truck. It was the first of August and the day was hot. A slight breeze and the openness of the truck bed made for a cooler ride.

Tizzie's place looked deserted, which it was. I hopped off the back of the truck and went around to the cab where Jess was holding the baby while Fannie climbed out of the front seat. She took Daniel from him and stood looking at the forlorn little house. "Oh, Jess. It's perfect," she said.

I wrinkled my brow and wondered if she was looking at the same run down house I was.

Jess shook his head, "It could use some sprucing up."

"Let's go inside," she said.

The three of us walked up onto the uneven porch and Jess opened the door. I stood in the parlor. Do you want me to hold Daniel while you look around?" I asked.

Fannie placed him in my arms. "Thanks, Vallie."

She and Jess wandered to the kitchen and into the two bedrooms. "What more could we want?" I heard her say. One thing I knew about Miss Fannie, she wasn't into the fancy way of life.

"Now, Fannie. I've got to check out the land to see if it can be productive. Doesn't look to me as though there's been any crops grown on it for a long time."

"You go explore. Vallie and I can sit on the porch while you do."

There were two rockers on the porch where we each took a seat after I dusted them off with my handkerchief. Baby Daniel had woken up and was ready for his lunch. We talked while she nursed her baby.

"What do you want to do with your life, Vallie? Lots of girls your age are married with children."

"That's a question I've been asking myself," I answered. "I don't even have a boyfriend. I expect my sister may be married sometime soon. That will make Mother happy."

"Mothers think their daughters should be married for security. I grew up in Washington in a big family like yours. I worked as a waitress and cleaning houses. Addie and I lived in a boarding house while she worked for the Red Cross during the war.

That's when I met my husband and I was ready to get married. Maybe you should go to the city if you don't want a life on the farm."

I chuckled. "I wouldn't know what to do in the city. Miss Eva Lou, Miss Tizzie's cousin, invited Luke and me to visit her in Washington."

"Luke?" asked Fannie.

Then I laughed. "He's my brother. He has dreams of being a big league baseball pitcher."

"You should both go, and take in a Washington Senators ball game while you're there." Daniel had finished nursing and she was burping him on her shoulder when Jess came driving the truck over a bumpy dirt path.

"What's the verdict?" She hollered as the truck stopped.

He leaned out the open window. "It's going to take a lot of work." He got out of the truck and came onto the porch. "It depends on how much she wants for it because we're going to need to buy farm equipment."

"We've got money saved up." she said.

"We'll need a truck, tractor, wagon, horses, cattle, and the list goes on," came his dejected reply.

"We'd need that anyway," countered Fannie. "You could borrow from the bank and pay the loan off with the money you get from leasing out those gravel pits you bought in California."

I was beginning to feel uncomfortable listening to what was none of my business.

Then Jess smiled. "You really like this place, don't you?"

Fannie threw him a kiss. "I can make it a home."

Jess cocked his head to the side. "Well then, Miss Fannie, we shall talk with Tizzie Nelson."

I was glad to have that conversation over. I stood up. "Do you need a drink of water before we head back?" I asked.

They both nodded. I went into the kitchen and pumped water from the well, rinsed three glasses, filled them with the cold refreshing water and took them to the porch.

We drank in silence. I knew they were both thinking about what they could do with this place.

When we finished, I took the glasses back into the kitchen and left them in the sink.

The Edwards were in the truck. I climbed in the back and we were headed home.

We were right on time for the meal Nora and Mother had prepared.

Father and the boys had cleaned up, and Mother invited Jess and Fannie to wash their hands before we ate, if they wanted to.

"Thank you, Mrs. Brown. Our hands touched a lot of dusty spots," said Fannie.

"Houses can change that way when they're not lived in," replied Mother. "We have set places for you at the end of the table."

Baby Daniel lay on a blanket on the sofa in the parlor. He was fast asleep.

When we all sat down, Father said grace and everyone was introduced to the Edwards. Father knew Jess from dealings with Lockwood. Fannie fit in as though she had known us for years.

Father posed the question after we had filled our plates with roast beef, potatoes, green beans and fresh tomatoes. "What do you think of the place, Jess?" he asked.

Jess finished swallowing a sip of iced tea. "I'm sure you realize there's been some overgrazing, but not to the point it isn't salvageable. It will take time and hard work to get it back into condition."

"I love the house," Fannie said. "The little stream nearby will be enough that I can put in a vegetable garden and flowers around the front. With some new paint, a new roof and the sagging porch jacked up, it will be what I have wanted."

Mother smiled at her. "I have some spring bulbs you can have and plenty of vegetable seeds. Nora and I like to garden."

I noticed Mother didn't include me. I was the complainer when it came to canning pickles, tomatoes and whatever else Mother wanted to set aside for the winter months. I guess I disliked vegetable gardening as much as Luke detested haying season.

Perhaps Miss Fannie was right. Maybe Luke and I should go to Washington and visit Miss Eva Lou. It wasn't that I wanted to spend time with the prissy lady, but it would be a place to stay. In a couple weeks the farm would be awash with chores. I wondered if Mother and Father would consider Luke and me venturing into the city we had never been to.

Chapter 25

Tizzie Nelson lived four days after she had met Jess and Fannie Edwards and their baby. It was long enough to have the lawyer come from Berryville to transfer the Nelson farm to the Edwards.

Tizzie sold it for one dollar with the stipulations that she would be buried on it and Jess and Fannie would live there for at least twenty-five years and make it a working farm.

That was more than satisfactory to Jess and Fannie. They told her of their plans for the place, which made a happy death for Miss Tizzie.

Her funeral was held at Stone's Chapel with Reverend Stephens officiating. To my surprise, Windy Wendell made it a short farewell. What else could he do? Tizzie was not much of a church-going lady. What Reverend Stephens knew was what Mother had told him and it was her idea to have a funeral in the chapel.

Miss Eva Lou did not attend. She sent a card to Mother thanking her for all she did for her cousin with no laments about Tizzie's passing. I wondered if Miss Eva Lou was miffed because Tizzie didn't leave the farm to her. My nineteen-year-old mind did a lot of wondering.

After the funeral, the women of the church held a dinner outside on the lawn. I was sitting by myself watching Lucy and Davey play with other children, when I saw Ashton Corbin coming toward me.

My heart did a flip. I wasn't sure why he affected me that way, but he did. "Hi, Ash," I said, acting as though I saw him on a daily basis.

"Hello, Val."

Val? No one had ever called me that. I rather liked the sound of it.

"What are you doing here?" Wasn't that a silly question.

"Uncle Vern and Aunt Elsie said it was important to pay respects to those who have died in the community. Did you know Mrs. Nelson?" he asked. He sat down on the ground next to me.

I nodded. "I used to work for her, cleaning her house and whatever else she needed done."

"What was she like?"

I had to think a minute before I answered. "She was a crotchety old woman with a heart of gold."

Ash laughed. "I missed you while you were gone. I thought I might see you over at the Lockwood farm, but we never got there."

"What have you been doing? Luke says you don't come to church regularly." I knew that was a leading statement the moment I uttered it.

He smiled at me. "You've been asking about me?"

I felt my face flush. "Just curious," I replied. "I didn't go to church when I was working at Lockwood."

He picked up a twig and tossed it away. "I've been going to baseball games and playing in some."

"I didn't know you liked baseball. My brother Luke has dreams of being a big league pitcher. He's always practicing trying to throw crab apples through a knothole in the fence."

Ash chuckled. "That's a good way to develop an eye for the plate. I used to be a pitcher for my college team. I miss it."

"Miss Fannie said Luke and I should go to Washington and watch the Senators play."

"Who is Miss Fannie?" he asked.

"She's a wonderful lady. She and her husband have bought Tizzie Nelson's place. They're going to fix it up and run it like it should be run. Miss Fannie lived in Washington. She said because I don't know what I want to do, I should go and see what the city is like."

He looked at me under hooded brows. "You've never been to Washington?"

I shrugged a shoulder. "I've never had reason to."

"I've lived there all my life," he said. "I could show you around."

That made my heart do a double flip. "I know a lady there who has invited us to visit."

"Us?" he asked.

"Luke and I. She's a cousin of Tizzie Nelson's and we helped her out when she came for a visit and Tizzie got sick."

"You could stay at our house," he offered. "We've got a big house."

I knew my parents would never agree to that, but they might let us go to Eva Lou's. They wouldn't have to know that Ashton Corbin was going to show us the city.

We had two weeks before the haying started. If I could talk them into letting us go, we could leave on Saturday morning and come home on a Sunday evening train. The wheels in my head were turning. With permission from my parents and Eva Lou, we could go next weekend.

I turned my head to look at him. "Will you be there next weekend?"

He nodded. "There's going to be a good baseball game."

"What if Luke and I can go?"

He thought a moment. "I'll tell you what. If you can, I'll pick you up so we can all ride the train together. I can get you wherever you need to go. We can have a great time."

His enthusiasm carried me away, until I thought about how I was going to get my parents to agree. I could still put in my two days at Lockwood, and I did have plenty of money for Luke and me.

Lucy and Davey came running over to where we were sitting. "You're supposed to show me how to skip stones," Davey said.

"Well, let's go," Ash replied.

The children ran ahead and we followed to the small pond on the other side of the chapel. I saw Mother look up as we walked away.

I was sure Mother thought that Ashton Corbin was above the status of us farm people.

142

Perhaps that was because of how he dressed and carried himself in a self-assured way. To me, I found him to be very nice, and I wanted to get to know him better.

I decided to invite him to our house for supper. I might as well be honest with my parents because they would find out anyway if we meet Ash in Washington.

As he was teaching Davey how to sidearm the flatter stones, I said, "Ash, would you like to come for dinner this evening?"

"What time?"

"We usually eat at six."

"Okay," he said. "I'll be through helping Uncle Vern by then. You'd better get your mother's permission."

"Oh, she won't care. We always have enough food for visitors."

He came over to me and smiled. "I like that. My mother has to have a week's notice if someone is coming for dinner so she can prepare a menu for the cook."

Ashton's mother has a cook? Perhaps his home was like Lockwood where Peg was the cook and general maid. He said his house was big.

People were leaving, so we took Lucy and Davey back to where the women were cleaning up and the men putting away tables.

"Mother, I don't think you've met Mr. Corbin's nephew. This is Ashton. I've invited him to dinner this evening."

Mother's puzzled look turned into a smile. "We can always set another chair at the table," she said.

"Thank you, Mrs. Brown. I'm pleased meet you. I don't wish to be an intrusion."

"Of course not," Mother replied.

I was pleased. I felt confident that after she and Father had a chance to talk with him, they would allow Luke and me to go to the city.

Ash spotted his relatives ready to leave. "Please excuse me," he said. "I see it's time to go," and he hurried off to join his uncle.

After Ash was gone, Nora said, "I like him, Vallie. Billy Wood is coming to dinner, also."

Mother continued cleaning up, "I don't think those two will have much in common," was her remark.

Chapter 26

The evening Ashton and Billy Wood came for dinner went well. Father asked Ashton about his family and what his plans were when summer was over. Ashton said his father had a responsible position in the government and wanted Ash to work in a government job. Ash said his plans were uncertain at this time, but he would be returning to Washington after Labor Day.

When the subject of spending the weekend in Washington with Eva Lou came up, Mother raised her eyebrows and looked over at Father.

He cleared his throat. "That doesn't sound like a good idea. You two young people know nothing about a big city."

Ash was quick to speak up. "I know the city well, Mr. Brown. I can take them around. We could take in a Senators game. They have a good team and may get to the World Series. Walter Johnson will be pitching."

Luke almost jumped out of his chair. "Walter Johnson? I'd love to see him pitch."

"We could stay with Miss Eva Lou. She has invited us," I said.

"I haven't received further word from her," said Mother.

"I'm sending a letter. Her reply should be back by Tuesday or Wednesday." That's what I prayed for.

Billy Wood surprised all of us by saying, "It's good to give the city a try. I could go through the Smithsonian a few more times."

Fortunately, Ash said, "That's a great place."

Otherwise, I think you could have heard our jaws drop. Billy Wood had been to Washington?

Lucy asked for another piece of cake.

Father looked at me and said, "We'll discuss this later."

We had discussed it after Ash left, Father, Mother, Luke, and I. Mother was against it, but Father prevailed and said if Eva Lou agreed we could go. He even said he trusted Ashton to make sure we were in safe places.

That meant we had to wait for a reply, but Luke and I were both excited at the thought of a big adventure.

Chapter 27

I was cleaning Miss Addie's bedroom when I heard visitors downstairs. It sounded like Miss Fannie. I knew Miss Gilbert was in with the babies. If Miss Addie asked her to bring the babies downstairs, I could hurry and clean the nursery without having to meet the nanny. I don't know why I didn't care for her, but I didn't and I don't think Miss Peg did either. Perhaps it was because she gave the impression that she was on a higher plain in life than I was. It was the same discomfort I had in the presence of Mr. Alex.

Miss Addie did ask for the babies to be brought downstairs and after the nursery was quiet, I hurried to clean it before I went down to the kitchen.

"Vallie, Miss Adelaide has asked for tea and sandwiches. Can you fix the tea while I get this tray ready?" asked Peg.

"Do you want the porcelain or the china tea pot?"

"China keeps the tea warmer," she answered. "Miss Fannie is here with the baby. You know, Vallie, I will have to talk to Mr. Alex because I am getting worn out. I'm afraid, I'll have to leave if he doesn't hire another helper." Peg sounded tired.

"Doesn't Miss Gilbert help?"

Peg looked over at me and made a sour face. "That woman expects to be waited on as though she is royalty."

Now that Miss Tizzie was dead, I hoped they weren't going to ask me to fill in the busy times. "I think you should talk to him," I said.

I prepared the tea and Peg asked me to take it to the parlor. I didn't mind because I wanted to see the babies, Miss Addie and Miss Fannie. I put on a clean apron before I went in.

"Vallie," said Miss Addie. "How nice to see you."

"It's my day to be here," I replied.

Fannie spoke up, "I was just telling Addie how lucky we were that you told us about the Nelson place. Jess says we can move into the house next month. We'll be neighbors."

I smiled at the thought. "That will be good."

Miss Gilbert sat rocking a big carriage that held the twins. They were fast asleep. I could tell the nanny was taking in every word of the conversation while pretending not to. I also felt her eyes watching me as I served. What was she thinking?

Fannie was holding Daniel and Addie looked bright and smiling. She said to Fannie, "Alex has agreed that I can get back to the bookkeeping now that Miss Gilbert is here. I have to be busy other than taking care of the babies."

I poured the tea into rose decorated china teacups. The women helped themselves to the chicken salad sandwiches.

"You do like that kind of work," said Fannie. "That's what you went to school to learn."

Addie nodded her head. "Vallie that might be something you might be interested in. You could go to secretarial school like I did."

"Miss Addie, I don't think I would be a good secretary."

"Vallie needs to do something with those sketches she does," chimed in Fannie. "They are a work of art."

I blushed at the compliment, but I knew that was something I did with my spare time. Unless Irene Butler wanted them for her seamstress shop, they were only a pile of papers.

"Miss Fannie, Luke and I may go to Washington next weekend. You said we should visit the city."

They both looked at me. Miss Addie said, "I think that is the best idea I've heard. It is good to get out into the world. We can always come home."

"That's true," said Fannie. "If you go, find an Irish pub and eat some fish and chips."

Addie shook her head. "I don't recommend that on your first time in Washington. That is unless you take Fannie with you. She knows the places to go and they know her."

Fannie just laughed aloud.

Then they began talking about their babies and I left the room.

"The tea and sandwiches are served, Miss Peg. If there isn't anything else, I'll be on my way.

"You go ahead, Vallie. I'll see you on Monday if I survive."

I couldn't help but smile as I took off the apron, picked up my tote bag and went out to saddle Ches for the ride home. This had been a good day, and I looked forward to next week.

Chapter 28

It was set. Miss Eva Lou sent a note to Mother that she would be glad to have Luke and me come for the weekend. Ash said he had a car so he would drive us to Washington and back saving us train fare.

Mother, as I suspected, was not pleased with the whole affair. She lectured me about keeping my feelings neutral regarding Ash. "You'll get hurt if you get too close. He will be leaving soon, find a girl more suited to his station in life."

She warned us about the dangers that lurk in a big city, how to behave at Miss Eva Lou's, and be sure our money was tucked in a safe place.

Father just told us to keep our heads on straight. He trusted Ashton to be a sensible guide. "Vern wouldn't agree with this if he didn't trust his nephew."

Ash had never driven a car to church so I didn't know what to expect. He'd said his uncle thought it was best to leave it parked at the farm.

Early Saturday morning, I caught my breath when I saw a yellow coupe coming down the lane with yellow spoke wheels, a rumble seat and spare tire behind. I had seen such cars in magazines.

"Look at that, Vallie! We'll ride in style." Luke was as excited about this trip as I was. His

151

dark eyes sparkled, and I had to admit that my sixteen-year-old brother with his six foot frame and toned body was a good looking young man.

The area girls tried to get his attention, but Luke's interest was baseball. Ash Corbin shared Luke's desire to pitch in the big leagues, but I was sure Ash would go into a profitable government position as his father told him there was no money in sports. As for Luke, I doubted he would ever leave the farm.

I was dressed in a lilac flowered cotton dress and my Sunday straw hat. My satchel carried what I needed for the overnight stay. I knew the time would pass quickly and we would be back home too soon. Undaunted, I determined to make the most of it.

Of course, all of my family was out admiring Ash's car and ready to see us off. Ash said the automobile was a gift from his parents for his graduation.

Mother looked at me and raised an eyebrow. That fact only solidified her worry that I might come to care for Ash. I wasn't naive. I knew who I was and where I fit in. However, I liked being with him. He was nice, and if he wanted to show me and my brother his knowledge of the city, that was fine with me.

I was the last one to come out of the house. Ash smiled at me, took my satchel and placed it behind the bench seat. He was dressed in a casual checked shirt and tan trousers.

"We can all three ride in the front," he said.

"How about the rumble seat, Ash? Could I ride there?" asked Luke. "I want to see the sights on the way." Luke wore a straw hat and long-sleeved cotton shirt.

"If you think you're going to be comfortable," Ash answered. "It might get too warm as the sun gets up in the sky."

"If it does, I'll wrap on the back window." The rumble seat was open and he climbed in with his small bundle of what he would need and placed it under the trunk area.

Mother handed me a box for Eva Lou. "I've sent her some cookies, strawberry jam and pickles so don't drop it."

Then Nora handed me a small basket. "These are ham sandwiches, cheese, and treats for your lunch." She hugged me and said, "Have a wonderful time."

It was hugs all around before Ash opened the door for me to step on the running board and take my seat.

"Ash, Lucy and me want to ride in that place where Luke is," said Davey.

Ash picked him up and whirled him around. "We'll see about that when we get back."

He tipped his hat to Mother, shook Father's hand and promised to get us home safely.

He got behind the wheel, pulled the choke, turned the key in the ignition, pushed in the clutch, put it in gear, and we were off.

We hadn't gone far when he looked over at me and said, "I envy you, Val. You have a great family."

I looked back at him and said, "Yes, I do."

The side windows were rolled down to let air circulate in the car. "When we stop for lunch, I'll roll the windshield open and that will make the afternoon pleasant," Ash said. Then he leaned out his side window and hollered, "How are you doing, Luke?"

"I couldn't be better," he hollered back. "How fast does this thing go?"

"Too fast for these roads. We'll get there in good time."

We had wound our way through Pine Grove, over the mountain, traveled through Bluemont and Round Hill before Ash decided to stop in Purcellville to put gas in his car. "This is my usual stop," he explained. "I'll fill up and we'll get the rest of the way. Would you care for a soda? Or, they have a drinking spout next to the well."

"I'd like to get out and walk a bit," I said. "Which way to the water?"

"I'll take you," he replied.

The gas station operator came out to the car in his oily overalls.

"Fill it up, please," said Ash.

The man grunted and opened the lid to the gas tank.

"Luke, come on," I said. "Let's get a fresh drink of water."

The three of us walked to the side of the small station where Ash showed us how to work the spout.

My first attempt threw water in my face causing Luke and Ash to laugh aloud, but I got the hang of it. The cold fresh water woke me up. I hadn't slept well and we had left the house before seven o'clock.

My accident with the water spout must have inspired my companions because they started fooling around trying to spray each other by sticking their fingers on the spout.

I stood back and after a moment said, "If you four-year-olds are ready, it's time to get back in the car." I could see the station operator placing the hose back on the pump.

"You're a spoil sport, Vallie," said Luke. However, he and Ash both took a healthy drink and we headed back to the car.

Ash and I didn't converse much. I was busy taking in the hamlets and towns we passed through and he concentrated on driving, avoiding ruts, wagons, horses and other vehicles. It was slow going through Leesburg and I wondered if we should have taken the train. Ash was a good driver and he knew the road well. Everything was new to me. If he saw a site that had some importance, he would point it out to me. I liked that.

At Goose Creek, he knew a spot where he could pull the car off the road and we could have lunch. He had a blanket behind the seat, which he spread on the ground and I brought out the basket Nora had prepared.

The sandwiches and slices of cheese were wrapped in wax paper. The treats were chocolate cream puffs. Nora was good at baking, and I appreciated her thoughtfulness in seeing that we had a free lunch.

I could tell that Luke, after seeing Ash as too fancy for the farm set, had taken a liking to him. Perhaps it was their mutual interest in pitching baseball. The evening Ash came to our house for dinner he had showed different pitches that he had learned from his college days. "Keep practicing," he had said to Luke. "You're good enough to pitch college ball."

After eating, we rinsed our hands off in the creek and wiped them on the napkins Nora had packed in the basket. We climbed back into the car and were on our last leg of the journey.

Ash said, "You still okay in the back, Luke, or do you want to come up front?"

"I'm fine as long as the car keeps moving," Luke replied.

A third person in the front seat would have made a cramped ride and I would be stuck in the middle, so I was glad that Luke wanted to remain in the rumble seat.

We rode along the Potomac River and crossed the Key Bridge on our way into the city. Ash explained the bridge was named for Francis Scott Key and was opened a year ago.

I was in awe of the whole panorama: the river, the bridge, Georgetown way up on a hill to my left and the buildings of the city before me. I was seventy-five miles from home and in a different world. It was no wonder Miss Adelaide and Miss Fannie said I should take this trip.

Ash had the address for Eva Lou and had no trouble in finding the brick townhouse where she lived. I am not sure what I expected, but it wasn't a row of houses all hooked together.

When Ash parked at the side of the street, Luke hopped out of the rumble seat in a flash. He opened my door. "Vallie, what do you think of this place? I've never seen so many people, buildings, and cars. Wait 'til I get home and tell Mark about this!"

While Luke was beside himself with wonder, I had butterflies dancing around in my stomach. As I stepped onto the running board, I saw Miss Eva Lou open the door and step out onto the stoop. A low wrought iron fence surrounded the small front yard.

Ash retrieved my case and opened the low gate. Miss Eva was waving her handkerchief in a greeting. "Come right in," she said. "I've been waiting for you."

I introduced Ashton Corbin. She was all atwitter at our arrival, and I was glad we had come. She made us feel like a bright spot in her quiet life.

Ash told her that he lived in Washington with his parents on K Street. That seemed to impress her. He told her that he would like to take us all to dinner at the Willard Hotel, if she had not made other plans.

She actually clapped her hands together. "Ashton, I haven't been to the hotel in a long time. Of course, we will go." Then she looked at us. "You young people are in for a treat."

"I'll be back at five. We can show our visitors some of the sights of the city." Eva agreed and Ash left.

"I am so happy that you decided to come," she said to Luke and me. "Your bedrooms are upstairs. I don't climb the stairs anymore, but my maid has assured me they are ready for visitors. You go ahead up, while I fix us some nice cold tea. It is a long tiring trip from where you live."

We took our small travel bags up the stairs. There were two cozy rooms with a bathroom between them. I took the room to the right.

Luke opened the door to the bathroom and I heard him catch his breath. "Wow! Vallie, we've got indoor plumbing!" He kept his voice to a loud whisper for which I was grateful. Luke had a tendency to be over exuberant.

Each room held a small bureau, rocker, secretary's desk and straight chair. There was even a closet in each. We unpacked what we had brought and went downstairs where Miss Eva Lou had set our tea on a table on the back porch. Her back lawn was not bigger than the front, but she had made lovely small gardens and the flowers of summer were in bloom.

I gave her the box Mother had sent. She seemed quite pleased at all of the items, especially the popcorn. "I can pop real farm grown popcorn," she said.

Luke looked over at me and raised an eyebrow as if to say, "What other popcorn can there be?"

We chatted small talk about how things were on the farm, how sad it was that Tizzie died, and how thankful she was that we had cared for Tizzie. I told her about Jess and Fannie buying the Nelson place, but I didn't tell her the terms. Miss Eva looked at the watch she wore around her neck and announced it was time for us to get ready for Ash to return.

I had brought a dress to wear to church, so I thought that would be more appropriate than the blouse and skirt I was wearing. We took our tea glasses into the kitchen and went upstairs to change.

I combed my hair and smiled at myself in the mirror. This weekend was going to be one to remember.

Chapter 29

At five o'clock, as he had promised, Ashton Corbin drove up in a different car than the sporty coupe we had arrived in.

"Holy cow, Ash. Where did you get this?" asked Luke as he walked around to check out the big black sedan.

"It's my dad's car," answered Ash. "He let me borrow it for this evening."

It did occur to me that there was no way he could fit Miss Eva, himself, Luke and me into the coupe.

I was pleased. Ash and Miss Eva could sit in the front seat while Luke and I would sit in the back. It was a handsome automobile with a white top and white trim around the tires. Everything was polished and glistened in the afternoon sun.

Ash escorted Miss Eva to the car and assisted her into the front seat. Luke surprised me by acting the gentleman and opened the back door for me. Inside the seats were plush velvet.

Luke leaned over and whispered in my ear, "This sure beats riding in a wagon."

I looked over at my brother and smiled.

Ash did take us on a tour. He drove streets holding restaurants, department stores and business offices. We saw buildings of the Supreme Court, the Capitol, the Smithsonian, and the White House before we ended up at the Willard Hotel.

"There is too much to see, but I think we hit the highlights," Ash said as we alighted the car and stood on the sidewalk taking in what we could.

He took Miss Eva's arm as we walked up the steps to the hotel where a Doorman welcomed us at the entrance. "It's going to be a lovely evening," he said.

"Yes, it is," Ash answered. We stepped inside and Luke gave me a questioning look. We were definitely out of our element.

The whole place smelled of influence. Never the less, Luke and I followed Ash and Miss Eva as the waiter showed us to a table Ash had reserved.

The waiter seated Miss Eva while Ash held the chair for me before he and Luke took their seats. The dining room was crowded and there was a steady hum of quiet conversations. Ash and Miss Eva seemed right at home, but I could not relax and I was sure it was the same for Luke.

Ash ordered a carafe of wine. There were wine glasses on the table along with water glasses and cups and saucers. I was stumped at what all of the utensils were for, so I decided I would keep an eye on Ash and Miss Eva and follow their lead. I hoped Luke would do the same so that neither of us looked too out of place.

The high-ceilinged dining room was adorned with crystal chandeliers that sent out sparkled light. All tables held white tablecloths and a lighted candle. The long narrow windows were hung with long silk drapes.

The thought did occur to me that Ashton Corbin was showing off for a couple of naive country folk, but I didn't want to think that.

Then two fashionable young ladies stopped as they were going to the powder room. "Ashton! Where have you been? We miss you at our parties," the more attractive of the two said.

Ash stood up. "I've been spending the summer in the country," he replied.

Luke stood also using his manners.

The two young women gave me and Luke a cursory glance. "Yes, I can see that," said the bolder of the two while the other gave a flirty smile to Luke.

Ash didn't have time to introduce us before they turned to leave. "Hurry back, darling Ashton," the first girl called over her shoulder.

Ash and Luke sat down. We were all embarrassed even Miss Eva Lou.

"Such rude girls," was her comment.

"They were classmates," said Ash as he looked over at me with an apologetic half smile.

It was an uncomfortable few seconds before the waiter brought the wine. Ash took a sip and approved of it so our four glasses were filled by the waiter. Ash held his glass up in a toast, "To newfound friends," he said and we all clinked our glasses. I had tried wine before and it wasn't to my liking, but I took a sip and found this to have a smooth, pleasant taste.

As for Luke, I knew alcohol wasn't a stranger to him because he and his friends would sneak a bottle of hard cider on special occasions. One of those little secrets brothers and sisters keep from their parents.

I took a couple more sips of wine and felt less uptight. I hadn't eaten since lunch and wondered if the wine had more of an effect on an empty stomach.

When the waiter brought the menus, Ash asked if there were any specials this evening. There were. Miss Eva Lou and I settled on the chicken dish while Ash and Luke chose the beef.

"The ball game is at one o'clock tomorrow," Ash said to Luke. "I'll pick you up at noon. Have everything packed because we'll have to leave right after the game. Are you coming with us, Val?"

"Of course you should go," Miss Eva said to me. "There is nothing like being in the crowd at the ball park. When my husband was alive, we went as often as we could."

I could not picture this dainty woman at a baseball game. "I thought you lived in southern Virginia," I said.

"We had a home and his relatives down there, but I was born in Washington and I kept the house. My husband was a business man so we came up frequently." She let out a deep sigh. "But, he's gone, his relatives are gone, Tizzie is gone, and I have one niece living here. That's the reason I moved back."

I couldn't help but feel sympathy for her. I thought how fortunate I was to have my family.

"I think it would be good to go to the game. That way we can leave right from the ball park.

What time do you think we will be back home?"
I asked.

"I expect around eight o'clock," Ash said.

The waiter brought our food. It was just in time because I had taken a few more sips of wine and was beginning to feel light headed.

On the way back to Miss Eva's, Ash asked if we wanted to stop at a candy shop and take some home. I thought that a splendid idea. A box of fudge would make everyone happy.

The little shop was in the basement of a building. We went down the stairs while Miss Eva elected to stay in the car. There were fudges of every description. I bought mixed boxes of chocolate, vanilla, butter pecan, marshmallow, peanut butter, maple nut. Four small boxes for the people at Lockwood and two large boxes for home. All in all I paid nine dollars because I bought a fancy tin for Eva and one for Ash. It was the least I could do for all their kindness.

When we got back to the townhouse, it was close to eight o'clock. Miss Eva asked if he would like to come in for a cup of tea, but Ash declined.

"Thank you for asking," he said, "Tomorrow is going to be a busy day, so I'd better be on my way."

Luke had the key and he was opening the door for Miss Eva while I walked to the car with Ash. "This has been a most enjoyable evening," I said. "We'll be ready when you come tomorrow."

He looked down at me and smiled. "I'd like to take you dancing, Val" he said.

I felt a wave of pleasure at his smile and I liked it when he called me Val. I think I would be close to heaven dancing with Ash, but I heard my mother's voice say, "Don't get too close, he'll find a girl more in his stature of life."

I tried to return his smile. "I'll see you tomorrow," I said. Then with a twinge of sadness, I watched as Ashton Corbin drove away.

Once inside the house, Miss Eva said, "He's a very nice young man."

"Yes, he is," I replied.

Chapter 30

That same evening, Nora Brown was thinking of Vallie and Luke. The farm house didn't seem the same without them.

Nora was waiting for Billy Wood. There was a band concert in Berryville and Billy liked music. It didn't matter what kind.

Using one of Vallie's sketches, she fashioned a dress to wear. It was made of a thin green and gold striped material with an insert of white lace in the bodice and tiny gold buttons around the square neck. Nora looked in the mirror in her upstairs bedroom. She wished Vallie was here to give her opinion, although Nora was pleased with her reflection.

The big test would be if she could pass her mother's inspection. Nora was sure of many things, but not when it came to fashion. That was Vallie's realm and she was good at it.

With a heavy sigh, Nora picked up her cloth pouch that matched her dress and left the room. She hesitated before entering the kitchen.

Mrs. Brown was working around the sink and turned when Nora entered. She didn't say a word as she stood staring at her oldest daughter.

Nora could feel the palms of her hands beginning to perspire. Her mother said, "Nora, you look lovely. Would you like to wear my gold stickpin? I think it would be just perfect."

A wide smile graced the face of Nora Brown. She had passed inspection with the offer of wearing her mother's prize piece of jewelry.

When Billy arrived, he did a double-take, but he waited until they got in the truck to say, "I'm proud to take you to the concert. You'll be the best looking girl there. We need to get married."

Nora looked over at him and smiled. "We don't know each other that well."

"Sure we do," he said. "We've known each other almost since we were born. I told you before that I've had my eye on you, while you were wasting your time with Harold. We need to make up for lost time."

The reticent Nora Brown didn't answer. She sat quietly mulling over his words. She did know him well; she'd known him ever since they attended Bible study at Stone's Chapel. Billy was hardworking, had plans for the future, had simple tastes, and above all he was honest. They had similar likes. What more could a girl ask for? Especially one who was going to turn twenty-three.

She looked over at the rugged red-haired man beside her. "Perhaps you're right," she said.

Billy looked startled as he pulled the truck to the side of the road and turned off the engine.

"Do you mean it, Nora? Will you marry me?"

Nora looked at him and smiled. "People will think this is sudden, but you're right. We have known each other for a long time. If you're serious, yes, I will marry you."

167

"I have never been more serious in my life," he replied. Right there in the farm truck parked at the side of the road, Billy Wood kissed her full force. "As soon as I can get to the jewelry shop, I'll put a ring on your finger."

"Let's wait for the ring before we tell anyone," she said.

He agreed.

They held hands walking to and from the concert. It didn't hurt to let people see they were a couple. Between them there was a mutual feeling of admiration and respect.

When they arrived back at the farm, Billy said, "You have made me the happiest man in the world," before he gave her a long gentle kiss. "I'll see you get that ring before you change your mind."

Nora smiled up at him and shook her head. "I won't change my mind," and she kissed his cheek. "I promise."

Billy held her close and kissed her once again before she went into the house. She heard the big farm truck lumber down the lane.

Her parents were sitting in the parlor. Her father was reading the *Clarke Courier* and her mother was darning socks.

"Did you have a good time, dear?" her mother asked.

"I had a wonderful time," replied Nora.

"You look a little flushed," her mother said. "Do you feel well?"

"I feel fine," said Nora as she removed her mother's piece of prized jewelry. She looked at her hand undoing the pin and knew she would have her own prize jewelry before long.

As Nora got ready for bed, she lamented Vallie wasn't here because she was bursting to tell someone. Of course, she and Billy agreed not to tell anyone, but Nora knew Vallie would keep her secret.

Chapter 31

Griffin Stadium was hot and humid on that August Sunday. I was glad for the wide brim on my straw hat and that I had worn my cotton blouse and skirt. Cotton was more breathable than some other fabrics.

Luke also had a wide-brimmed straw hat and he rolled the sleeves of his shirt up to the elbows.

Ash was wearing a green striped cotton shirt and light tan trousers. He also wore a wide-brimmed straw hat.

"I've brought a jug of ice water," he said. "We'll need it if we start to bake." He sat it behind his feet to keep it out of the sun.

Luke looked over at him, "Heck, this is just like haying season."

Ash laughed. "I plan to miss that. I'll be coming back here soon."

I sat between them. Hearing those words dampened my enthusiasm for the game about to be played, although I knew it was for the best. If I was around Ashton Corbin too often, I knew I would begin to care too much.

We had gone to a small Episcopal church this morning with Miss Eva. After church, she took us to a restaurant where she went every Sunday after services and had breakfast. She insisted on paying for it to our objections. However, she said it was her treat for us bringing some sunshine into her lonesome life.

What she had told me, and I couldn't help but think of it, as we waited for the game to begin, was that she had shown my sketches to a man who owned a small clothing factory.

"He designs clothes for the well-to-do. If you don't mind, I will give him your address so that he can send you a letter. He seems very interested in your ideas."

I had agreed Miss Eva could give him our address.

"Look, Luke. Walter Johnson is taking the mound. Pay close attention to how he pitches," Ash said. Then he looked at me. "Are you doing all right, Val? Let me know if you get too warm and we can get out of the sun for a while."

Both Luke and I were in awe of the mass of people in the stadium. It looked like all of Washington was in the stands. We sat behind third base where Ash said we might get lucky and catch a fly ball.

They were not a quiet crowd either. All during the game there were whistles, clapping, booing and catcalls. Before the game started the announcer introduced President Calvin Coolidge who was in a shady spot in a private booth behind home plate. He stood and doffed his hat, but he was too far away for us to see his face.

I can't say I was delighted with sitting in the hot sun watching men throw a ball around, but

I could see it was bringing joy to my companions. I was also quite a good actress, so I pretended I was having a great time while I sat there and sweat like Ches when I'd ridden him hard.

The water Ash brought was a godsend. It didn't stay ice cold but it was cooling and I could wet my handkerchief and dab my face and neck.

And, the most wonderful thing of all was in the ninth inning when a foul ball came our way, Luke reached out his long arm and caught it.

Mother was a big believer in Providence and after that small miracle, I was beginning to believe she was right. If Luke never made another game or became a big league pitcher, he had a souvenir to remember for the rest of his life.

It was cooler after the game when we walked back to the car, the same car we had ridden in from home.

"Let's get this thing moving so I can dry out in the wind," Luke said.

"I'll open the windows and the windshield so we can all dry out. Do you want to ride in front?" Ash asked.

"I'll take the rumble seat again," Luke answered.

"Let's get a sandwich to eat on the way. I've got a full tank of gas, which should get us back. I can't depend on a gas station being open on Sunday." Ash put what was left of the jug of water behind the front seat. "Come on," Ash said. "There's a little dive that's open after the game. My friends and I used to get a cold beer there. We can pick up something to eat."

He hooked his arm through mine as we crossed the street and a shudder of pleasure rushed through me.

We bought ham sandwiches, orange popsicles and Hostess cakes, which Ash paid for. I was going home with almost as much money as I had brought. We ate the popsicles right away and the cold sweetness felt soothing to my dry throat.

The sandwiches and cakes we took back to the car to eat on our way home. I had enough of the city crowds and hustling people. I wasn't sure Luke felt the same. He loved the trolleys and trains and shops.

Once we were on our way, Ash looked over at me and smiled his captivating smile. "Well, Miss Brown, are you ready to go back to your quiet life? There's a lot of this city I'd like to show you."

I looked at him and said, honestly, "I have had enough for now."

"I thought so," he said. "I think you're a country girl, Val."

I immediately became defensive, "Is that bad?"

"Not at all. I find you a refreshing change," he replied.

Those words raised hackles and I said, "I am not dumb and naive, Ashton."

He laughed. "I didn't mean that, Val. I find you puzzling."

"Puzzling? What does that mean?"

"It means that I haven't figured out how I feel about you," he said in a more serious tone.

"Figure me a friend. You'll be going back to Washington and on with your life." Wasn't I the stoic one?

He sighed, "Yeah, I haven't figured that out, either."

Near Purcellville, Ash pulled the car to the side of the road. "Let's eat our sandwiches here. We can sit on that knoll and be back on our way. It's going to be dark before we reach your place."

Luke was glad to stretch his legs and so was I. The air was pleasantly warm. Ash brought the jug of water and we sat on the grass.

I still had napkins Nora had sent in the picnic basket, so we ate both sandwich and cake, rinsed them down with water and were back on our way in less than fifteen minutes.

It was a quiet ride home. I think we were all tired. I knew Luke was because I looked out the back window and saw he was asleep.

I was happy to come over the mountain and see the street lights of Berryville in the distance. The town was a far cry from the streets of Washington, and even though it was around eight o'clock when we went through, it seemed as if the whole town was deserted.

"This is almost eerie," Ash said.

I had to agree with him. One night ago we had been leaving the Willard Hotel where there were plenty of people and plenty of lights. Some were on their way to the theater or a night club. It wasn't fair for me to make a comparison, but I did. Which did I prefer? I didn't know.

We drove down the farm lane about forty minutes later. The dim light emanating from the house gave me a warm feeling. It was good to be home.

Mother and Father were still up and came out the kitchen door. Then Nora and Mark appeared in their night clothes. The happy reunion woke Davey and Lucy, and they came running to me giving me a big hug.

There were hugs and handshakes all around. Ash was busy getting our belongings out of the car.

Father shook his hand. "Thank you for getting them back safely."

"Yes, sir." He said. "You're welcome. We had a good weekend."

"I'm sure we'll hear all about it," Father replied. "Would you like to come for dinner tomorrow evening?"

"Thank you, Mr. Brown. I'd like that. I'd better get on my way and catch Uncle Vern before he retires."

Out of the corner of my eye, I saw Ash open the door to his car. Mother and Nora were ushering the young ones back into the house and Father had come to talk with Luke.

I couldn't let Ash leave without saying goodbye, so I hurried to the car.

He turned and rested his hand on the top of the open door.

"Ash, I want to thank you for all you did for Luke and me. I think we would have been lost."

"You'd have done all right, Val. Your father has invited me to dinner tomorrow evening."

"Yes, I heard. Are you coming?"

"I wouldn't miss it," he said. "Maybe I'll solve my problem."

"Your problem?" I asked, thinking he meant about when to leave and return to his home.

"Yes," he said. He touched a finger to the tip of my nose. "You."

Then he smiled his wonderful smile, swung into the seat, and started the car.

He had thoroughly confused me.

"I'll see you tomorrow, Val," he called from the open window.

I couldn't say a word. I stood like a wood post and gave a weak wave of my hand. Ashton Corbin was beginning to disrupt my orderly way of life.

Chapter 32

The next morning I awoke to Nora shaking my shoulder. "Get up, Vallie. You're supposed to go to Lockwood today."

I groaned, sat up and rubbed my eyes to get the sleep out of them. "What time is it?"

"Past eight-thirty. You should have left over an hour ago."

I hugged my arms around my knees. "You look bright and cheerful," I said to my dear sister.

She put a finger to her lip and whispered, "I'm going to tell you something and you can't breathe a word of it."

"Cross my heart and hope to die," I replied, crossing my heart with my rosy-pink hand, my souvenir from the sun at the Senators game.

Nora whispered right into my ear, "Billy Wood asked me to marry him and I said yes."

I threw my hands up straight in the air. "When?"

"He's getting a ring at the jewelry store in Berryville as soon as he can. He may not be the most handsome man, but he is very nice, kind and considerate."

"I'm happy for you. He's a man of action, a far cry from Harold."

Nora nodded. "I guess I finally opened my eyes."

177

"It took you long enough," I said.

"If you're too tired, I can send Mark over to tell them you won't be coming."

I pushed the sheet aside and lowered my feet to the floor. "No, I need to go. I can explain why I'm late."

"I'll have Mark saddle Ches for you, and I'll make an egg sandwich you can eat on your way. Do you want coffee? I can put it in a Dixie Cup."

"Maybe the coffee will wake me up," I told Nora. "Just pour the coffee in a mug and I'll drink it before I leave."

Nora left our room and I hurried to get dressed for my day at Lockwood or what was left of the day.

Nora had the coffee ready for me when I came down the stairs. It was the right temperature so I could slug it down like a glass of water. For once Mother wasn't in the kitchen, so I missed my usual lecture: be careful, do a good job, and be home by dinner time.

I thanked Nora and Mark. He was waiting with Ches near the porch.

Ches snorted at me and nudged me with his head. I patted his neck.

"I think he missed you, Vallie," said Mark. "We all did."

Those words coming from my teen-aged brother made me smile.

"Luke will have to tell you all about it, if he hasn't already," I said. "I'll be back for dinner."

I climbed into the saddle, unwrapped my egg sandwich and urged Ches into a brisk walk.

Once I had the sandwich down, I could put him at a fast pace.

"Ches, it's good to be home. I think I have a busy day ahead." There was something comforting about talking to my horse.

When I arrived at Lockwood, Peg was hurrying around the kitchen like a chicken with its head cut off. "Am I glad to see you," she said, as I walked in the door. "That Miss Gilbert and I are going to come to blows if she keeps trying to boss me around."

"I thought you were going to talk with Mr. Alex about hiring another helper."

"I did, Vallie. He said he would take it under advisement."

That sounded like lawyer's speech to me. Was he really considering the request or just putting it off?

"I think you should talk to Miss Addie about it. I'm sure she doesn't realize what's going on." Didn't I sound like the wise one?

The older woman shrugged a shoulder. "Now that she's back doing the bookkeeping for the place, she doesn't have much time for small talk."

"I wouldn't call that small talk, Miss Peg." I reached into my tote and pulled out a small box of fudge. "Here," I said, holding out the box. "I brought you something to sweeten you up."

Peg stopped what she was doing. "Oh, my goodness. I forgot this was your big weekend in Washington. When we have time you can tell me about it."

179

"There isn't much to tell. We saw the buildings, ate at a fancy restaurant, and saw a big league baseball game. I liked indoor plumbing and the feel of silk sheets."

Peg had the box of candy open and was eating a piece. "This is delicious," she said, holding up the chocolate delicacy. "I've never slept on silk sheets."

I put my tote bag in the pantry, where I always put it.

The harried housekeeper finished the piece of fudge in four bites. "Mr. Alex is having four men in for lunch for a meeting of some kind. I've got the ham and chicken in the oven. I didn't know about it until this morning. I need you to peel the potatoes and shuck the corn."

"What time are they coming?" I asked.

"He said to have it ready by noon. The man has no idea how long it takes to prepare a meal for guests. I guess he thinks I just wave a magic wand." I had never seen Peg so flustered.

It was almost ten o'clock and no wonder Miss Peg was beside herself with worry.

"Miss Peg, if you have sweet potatoes, we could bake them in the oven and save the time of peeling. Baked yams go good with ham," I suggested. I only knew that because I had heard Mother and Nora discussing a meal.

"I thought of that, but there are no sweet potatoes." Then an idea came to her. "Vallie, you run on down to Lottie's and see if she has any we can use. She has a big garden. Tell her I'll repay her when we get new supplies from town."

180

I hurried down the path and found Miss Lottie outside working in her garden. I told her about Peg's dilemma and she was quick to help. "Vallie, you take these yams and some fresh tomatoes. I also made a big peach cobbler. Do you think Peg can use that? We're not going to eat it all, but I had to cook up the peaches."

I'm sure my smile was a mile wide. "Miss Lottie, I think you are going to make Miss Peg very happy."

Lottie smiled back at me. "Men don't understand how much time it takes to put a good meal together."

"Yes, ma'am. That's what Miss Peg said. You're right about that."

"Are you still doing your clothing sketches?" she asked.

I nodded. I wanted to tell her about what Miss Eva had said about showing them to a man who owned a small clothing factory, but it didn't mean anything so I didn't.

She put the sweet potatoes in the basket I carried then packed up the tomatoes and cobbler in a wood crate that had been cut down to make a tray. "I'll bring this back," I told her.

"That isn't necessary. I'll have Caleb pick it up when he's at the big house."

"Thank you, Miss Lottie. This food will take the worry off Miss Peg."

"I'm glad to do it. I hope the lunch turns out well."

Then I remembered the flowered box of fudge I had put in my apron pocket before I had left. "Miss Lottie I brought you a present from Washington."

Her eyes lit up with pleasure. "Vallie May, you are the joy of my day. You are going to have to tell me about your time in the big city." There was no hesitation on her part. She opened the box, took out a piece and took a bite. "I think I'll be selfish and keep it for myself," she said. "It will be my comfort on the difficult days."

I left her homey place feeling pleased.

When I went into the kitchen and showed Peg what Lottie had sent, I could see the lines of tension relax from her face.

"That sweet woman has saved the day," she declared. "Vallie, you go out and cut some flowers. Then you give the dining room a quick cleaning and set up the table."

If I was tired before I came, I thought I would be exhausted if this pace kept up.

Peg was kind to me. After we served lunch, she had me take a tray up to Miss Gilbert, who accepted it without a word. Taking the liberty of being in the nursery, I went to check on the twins. They were sound asleep and looked as though they had grown a bit. For all Miss Gilbert lacked in personality, she seemed to be taking good care of the precious babies.

I returned to the kitchen and Peg told me I could go on home. "The cleaning can wait until you come on Thursday, I know you are tired."

I felt instant relief and wasting no time, I retrieved my tote bag from the closet. "Thanks, Miss Peg. I am tired."

Leaving the house I stopped by the office and gave Miss Addie her box of fudge.

I could tell she was glad to see me and appreciated the gift I gave her. "Vallie you look as tired as I feel. You couldn't have brought me a more welcome present. One day I want to hear about your weekend."

On my way to get Ches, I went to the cabin where Jess and Fannie Edwards live. Miss Fannie greeted me with a big smile. "Well, if it isn't the wanderer back from the city."

"Hi, Miss Fannie. I brought you something." I handed her the box of fudge and she like the others opened it up.

"Yummy," she said. "I'll have to stop myself from eating it all at once. Valley May Brown you are a gem."

"Do you know when you are going to move into Miss Tizzie's place?" I asked.

"Just as soon as we get the outside fixed up. One of these days I want to hear about your stay in Washington."

I left Lockwood with a good feeling. My small gifts had brought some sunshine into their day. They all wanted to hear about my big venture into the city, and maybe someday I would tell them.

Climbing into the saddle, I said to my horse, "Ches, this day has turned out well, but I have one more hurdle to jump this evening."

This was the evening Ashton Corbin was coming for dinner.

Chapter 33

I wasn't sure Mother was too fond of Ash, but she put together a delicious dinner of roast beef and vegetables. Ash, being polite, thanked her and Nora for their delectable repast.

I didn't know if Mother didn't care for Ash or if she was concerned that somehow I might be hurt if he was around too often. Mothers seem to have a sixth sense when it comes to the welfare of their children.

I had noticed a change in Nora. She was more outgoing with a ready smile. There wasn't a ring on her finger, but I was sure Billy would be true to his word. I knew Mother noticed the change also because she would throw curious glances in Nora's direction.

After dinner, Ash and Luke went into the back yard to toss the baseball around. Ash played catcher while he gave Luke advice on different pitches. I watched from the back porch until I lost interest and pulled my paper and colored pencils from a drawer in an old chest.

While I was drawing, I heard Billy Wood's big truck come down the lane. He didn't come to the house as I expected, he went to the barn and I saw him talking to Father. Father had mentioned taking a sow and her piglets to the auction house.

Therefore, I assumed that was the reason for Billy's visit.

Of course, I felt sure he wouldn't leave without coming in to see Nora. He didn't disappoint me. Billy Wood had wasted no time in buying a ring and asking for Nora's hand.

Mother burst into tears when they told her, which brought Lucy and Davey into the kitchen all concerned about Mother crying. It wasn't long before we were all gathered in the kitchen with hugs and handshakes and well wishes. No date was set for the wedding. Mother would insist on a six month engagement so that people wouldn't talk about a shotgun wedding. That's just the way things were.

Ash came to my side and asked if I would like to go out for a walk, which we did.

"Val," he said, when we got to the path, "I'm leaving tomorrow."

I felt a tight knot in my throat. I had to swallow hard a few times before I could speak. "How long have you known this? You didn't say a word while we were in Washington."

"I didn't want to spoil the weekend. My father told me when I was home. He's secured a government position for me."

He reached over and took my hand. We walked on the path hand in hand and I thought I would swoon. I was glad it was dusk and the trees still shaded the path so that no one would see us.

"I only came for the summer," he said in an apologetic tone. "I guess my father thinks I've settled down."

"Is it what you want?" I asked.

He looked over at me. "You know it isn't, but I have an obligation to give it a try."

I made no attempt to take my hand from his. "Washington has a lot to offer. I'm sure you will become a successful business man."

He stopped walking and looked directly at me in the fading light of the sun. "Do you think you would like to give the city a chance, Val? We could have a good time together."

I shook my head. "I enjoyed our weekend in Washington, but I was glad to get home. Besides, what would I do? I am not one of the privileged young ladies I saw when I was there."

"I'm going to miss you," he said. "I wish you hadn't had to spend so much time at Lockwood."

At that moment, I wished I hadn't either.

"May I write to you or maybe come and visit some time?"

"I'd like that," I replied, but in my heart I doubted he would once he was back in the city. "I'm going to miss you, too. I don't think it was much of a summer for you," I said.

"It was a good time for me, Miss Vallie Brown. I wouldn't have met you or your family, and I might even seek out a small chapel when I need a place to sort out my thoughts."

I chuckled. "Windy Wendell didn't discourage you?"

"I've had a chance to talk to him. He's a nice guy, Val, and doing his best for his people." Ash replied.

186

Then he leaned over and gave me a quick kiss. "It's a kiss goodbye until I see you again," he said.

I was dumbstruck and it took me a few seconds to recover. "I do hope you find what you're looking for," I said.

We turned and walked back to the house as though nothing had transpired between us. But it had. The fact that he would be gone tomorrow perhaps was the hand of Providence at work. At least that's what Mother would say. Maybe she would be right. Still, that didn't lessen my wish that Ashton Corbin would stay right here.

When I went up to bed, Nora was lying on hers admiring the ring that sealed her future.

"Do you think Mother is pleased with the prospect of you getting married?"

Nora rolled on her side and looked at me. "I think so. She was always hoping I would marry Harold."

I plopped down on my bed. "I need to find a Billy Wood," I said.

Nora laughed. "You'd be bored to death. Ash Corbin likes you."

I lay back on the covers looking up at the ceiling, "For the summer, maybe. He's leaving tomorrow."

Nora sat up on the edge of her bed. "That's too bad. Are you sad?"

"A little," I lied. I knew if I said any more I would burst into tears.

"I'm going down for a glass of milk. Do you want anything?" she asked.

I shook my head. The minute she was gone, I slipped into my light cotton gown and retired for the night. With my face to the wall, Nora couldn't see the tears that silently fell.

Tomorrow would be another day.

Chapter 34

I was up around five the next morning. I could hear Mother and Nora already in the kitchen. It was going to be a hot August day and there would be plenty of work to do. I wanted none of that canning and pickling, so I decided I would do the wash. I figured Mother would be okay with that as long as I was busy with some worthwhile task.

Before I was up to my arms in wet clothes, I went down the front stairs, out to the pasture and brought Ches to the corral where I saddled him for a morning ride. I thought that would lift my spirits because I didn't want anyone to know how letdown I felt over the fact that Ashton Corbin was leaving today. I could be a pretty good actress when the time arose.

Father and my brothers were busy with their morning chores. I was careful to keep Ches away from view as I didn't want them questioning me about a ride this early in the morning.

"Ches, I will give you your breakfast when I get back, but we're going on a morning jaunt to clear my head."

I walked him down the lane before I got into the saddle and put him into a trot. Where I was going I wasn't sure. The morning air was cooler than the day promised to be and the cooler air was good for both Ches and me.

I just rode and was surprised to find myself at the pond next to Stone's Chapel. There was something about the spot that always gave me a comforting feeling. It was quiet except for the chirps of birds and faint sounds of farm life in the distance. I got off and let Ches drink from the pond while I gravitated toward the chapel. Not a soul was around that I could see.

I don't know what possessed me. I was drawn to peering into the chapel windows where I saw nothing but empty wooden pews. I spied our usual Sunday seats before my eyes wandered to where Ash had sat. I was wondering how it would feel to sit where he had when I almost jumped out of my skin.

"You're up early, Miss Brown. Is there something I can do for you?"

I turned with a gasp and came face to face with Reverend Stephens.

"I'm sorry if I startled you," he said.

It took me a moment to recover to the point where I could say, "We have a busy day ahead of us, so I am giving my horse some exercise before the heat of the day."

He offered a sly smile.

Then I felt a bit of irritation. What was he doing here this early anyway?

Windy Wendell wasn't much older than Nora. He wasn't married nor did he have a girlfriend, to my knowledge. For all I knew, maybe he didn't like women. I had heard that whispered. All of a sudden I felt uncomfortable, not only was I uncomfortable, I felt like a fool.

"I apologize for looking like a peeping Tom. I'm not sure why I'm here." The words tumbled out of my mouth.

Then he smiled. "Perhaps there is something weighing heavy on your mind. I often find solace here in the chapel."

I must have had a questioning look on my face because he quickly added, "The reason I'm here so early is because I left information I need for a nine o'clock presentation. I am not usually so forgetful."

The man was human after all. "I'm sure you have a lot on your mind."

"That I do," he replied. "I hear you and your brother spent a time in Washington."

That brought a bright smile to my face. "Yes. We had a grand two days and saw the sights. I was ready to come home."

He chuckled. "I know that feeling."

As we stood there, it dawned on me that I had never had a conversation with this man. Perhaps I should try to pay more attention to his sermons.

I believe I looked at him for the first time. He appeared younger as I studied his face, almost handsome, and more relaxed than when he was in the role of preacher. "I hope your meeting goes well," I said. "I need to be getting back to help with the chores."

Then he gave me a quirky smile and said, "I promise I won't tell your mother."

I could feel embarrassment creeping up from my toes. "Thank you," I replied and hurried to my horse who was patiently waiting and nibbling on some grass.

"Ches," I said. "I felt completely foolish. I'm nineteen years old and I should act my age. Now, every time I see that man I'm going to want to fall through a hole. Me and Windy Wendell with a secret between us? All of this happened because I didn't want to think about Ashton Corbin."

Ches turned his head toward me and snorted. There was nothing to do but climb into the saddle and head back to a day of mindless drudgery.

Chapter 35

My life didn't stop because Ash had gone back to Washington, and I continued to work at Lockwood. I could almost feel the strain in the air between Peg and Miss Gilbert. Even though Peg had threatened to quit, she remained at the estate where she was in charge of the big house. I don't know why she hadn't brought her cares to Miss Adelaide or why Miss Adelaide hadn't sensed the tension building between the two women. It was none of my concern, although their dislike of each other didn't make my job pleasant.

With any free time I had, I would go over to Tizzie Nelson's old place and help Miss Fannie. Little by little she and Jess were getting their house in shape. They still lived in the cabin at Lockwood, but it wouldn't be long before they could move into Tizzie's old house which sported a new roof, new front porch and new outhouse. Fannie was good at decorating and painting. If it came to sewing, she had no reservations about asking Miss Lottie to help.

I liked Miss Fannie. She was easy to talk to. My mind was becoming clouded with my feelings toward Ash, and the feud that was brewing between Peg and Miss Gilbert. I thought of Reverend Stephens asking if something was weighing heavy on my mind. I guess those thoughts qualified.

The land at the Nelson place had only been used for grazing and needed a lot of renewing. Jess Edwards had hired the three Sugg brothers to help get the land in shape. As long as they kept to the fields that was fine with me. I once heard Mr. Jess say to Fannie, "They may be a little slow in the head, but they're good workers." Maybe they were but you couldn't prove it by the looks of their place.

It was the first week in September when my life brightened. Billy Wood, who had become a fixture at the house now that he and Nora were officially engaged, brought two letters from town addressed to me.

He rose another step in my esteem for him because he handed them to me on the quiet. "I figured you might want to read them by yourself," he said.

My heart was beating like a drum when I went up to my bedroom, closed the door, and sat on the edge of my bed as I opened the first envelope. It was from Ash.

Dear Val,

I am hard at work here in Washington and not enjoying it one bit. The hours are long, the pay is good, and there is a chance for advancement. Yet, I am not pleased. Every spare minute I get, I find myself at the ball park either watching the Senators play or practice.

The World Series is next month and I have the feeling my

Senators are going to win. I wish that you and Luke could be here to see a game.

In fact, I wish you were here. I have been attending affairs that are meant to introduce me to important people, but I am not up to the Washington scene. I have lived here all of my life and never realized it until I spent the summer with my aunt and uncle. I guess my father was wise to send me your way.

Val, I know you and Luke understand how badly I want to be a big league pitcher. I have decided that next spring I am going to try out with the Senators. That's my secret and I know you won't tell anyone.

I will have given my father a chance at making me a respectable business man, but I am twenty-two and time doesn't wait.

I do miss you, more than I thought I would. I hope you miss me too. Once life settles down here, perhaps I can come out for a weekend. I long to breathe the pure country air.

I trust all is well with you and your family. You are fortunate.

Affectionately,
Ash

I sat there with the letter in my hand. He did say he missed me and hoped I miss him. What he doesn't know is that this letter has poignantly brought back the feeling of loss.

I tucked it into a private box I kept under the bed before I opened the second one which was short and to the point.

August 25, 1924
Dear Miss Brown,
I have closely examined the sketches Miss Eva Lou Nelson gave to me. Enclosed is a check for the two designs I plan to use.

If they are accepted, I will, with your permission, send you a contract to become a designer for my company.
Sincerely,
Channing Fox

I reached down and picked up the check that had fallen out when I opened the letter. Twenty-five dollars, I couldn't believe my eyes. Ten dollars for drawing sketches of clothing? And, he wants to send me a contract?

This seemed too good to be true. I decided to show the letter to my parents. Maybe I was growing up, because for once, this was a time when I felt I needed their advice.

Chapter 36

Father and Mother decided I should talk with Mr. Lockwood about the letter from Channing Fox. They said it was a matter for a lawyer and although he wasn't a lawyer anymore, he would know what to do.

The last thing I wanted to do was ask the advice of Alexander Lockwood. I always felt intimidated in his presence. That wasn't fair to Mr. Lockwood, but a person can't help the way she feels.

On Thursday, I stuffed the letter from Channing Fox into my apron pocket and headed to Lockwood for my usual day of work.

When I got there, I unsaddled Ches and left him in the corral while I picked up my tote bag and started for the big house. Something was different, although I wasn't sure what. Nevertheless, I walked up the path, onto the back porch and opened the kitchen door. Peg was always there to greet me, but not this morning. My immediate thought was that she had left as she had threatened to do.

Then I heard voices coming from the parlor: Mr. Alex, Miss Adelaide, the excited voice of Miss Peg and the high-pitched strained voice of Miss Gilbert.

I didn't mean to eavesdrop. However, the voices were loud enough that I got the gist of what had happened. It seemed Peg's displeasure with the nanny had boiled over to the point that she had thrown a plate of pancakes, grits and fried apples at Miss Gilbert. I couldn't help but smile to myself as I pictured the scene of the impeccable and perfectly coiffed nanny with the remains of breakfast splattered over her.

At that point Caleb Dunn, who must have heard the ruckus, came walking into the kitchen from the direction of the parlor. His face held a half smile. "You missed the big show, Miss Vallie. I believe you will have an interesting day ahead." Then he walked out the door and back to his duties as foreman of the Lockwood estate.

I didn't want an interesting day. I had planned on talking to Miss Adelaide about my problem in hopes that she would consult with her husband. Now, what was I going to do?

I heard Alex Lockwood's voice. He kept his tone even, but I could tell he was irritated. "This unfortunate incident could have been prevented if one of you ladies had come to me or Miss Adelaide with your complaints. If this news gets out, and it probably will, we will be the laughing stock of the county. By rights I should fire the both of you. After consideration, I have decided that your positions will continue on a trial basis for the next month. At that time I will assess the situation."

Then Miss Adelaide spoke up. "I'm sorry that I was unaware of the friction between you two. My concern is for my children and the upkeep of this house. Miss Gilbert, I have no complaints with your care for the babies. Neither do I have complaints about how you are caring for the house, Peg. I agree with my husband."

Of course the Lockwoods weren't going to discharge the two women because they needed their help. A month would give them time to find replacements, if replacements could be found.

I should have been getting the cleaning supplies out of the closet, but I stood mesmerized by the conversation coming from the parlor.

It was good I listened to what was decided as it involved me. Peg and Miss Gilbert would avoid contact with each other while I and the new cleaning girl Mr. Alex had recently hired, would act as go-betweens. That wasn't the news I wanted to hear. I had enough problems than to be pitched between two feuding women.

I took the cleaning supplies from the closet and hurried up the stairs. The first thing I did was go into the nursery and check on the babies. They were sound asleep. I was pleased to see that Anna was filling out and her skin was developing a healthy color. As for Alex, he was growing as a baby should. Had he taken nourishment from his sister before they were born? I knew that sometimes it happened with animals. It did make me wonder, but it didn't matter because any concerns I had held about Anna were gone as I looked down at the beautiful baby girl.

The rest of the day was quiet. Peg went about her duties without a word except to say hello. Miss Gilbert was aloof. Miss Adelaide called me into the office before I left and, without mentioning the upsetting incident, informed me of what I was to assume regarding my interactions with Peg and Miss Gilbert. At that time, I wanted to show her the letter from Channing Fox but I thought better of the idea. The whole house felt cold and uncomfortable. I wasn't sure I wanted to continue at Lockwood.

When I got home, Mother asked how my day had been. I told her it was the usual. Then she asked if I had shown the Fox letter to Mr. Lockwood. What could I say?

"No, Mother. There wasn't an opportunity," I responded.

"Well, that's too bad," she said. "These kinds of things need to be taken care of, Vallie May."

"Yes, ma'am," I replied and went up to my room where I pulled Ash's letter from my private box. I needed something to lift my spirits.

Chapter 37

I had spent the whole weekend mulling over the possibilities running through my mind. At Stone's Chapel on Sunday, I listened to the gospel and Reverend Stephens' explanation. Try as I did, after ten minutes into his sermon my mind began to wander. After the service I was standing aside waiting for Lucy and Davey, when Reverend Stephens came to me.

"Miss Brown, I'm pleased you are here. Did your early morning ride clear your thoughts?"

I wanted to fall through a hole. I gave a cursory glance around to see no one within earshot. "Yes," I replied. "It was a good day."

He smiled. "I have a favor to ask of you. Miss Stratton, our Sunday school teacher for the young ones, is going to be absent for a month, which leaves me in a bit of a bind. I wonder if you would be willing to fill in for her? I have seen that you are very good with the younger children."

The reverend had taken me by surprise. How could I answer him? In all honesty I could say no thank you. That would be too blunt, I thought, so I said, "Perhaps Nora would be a better choice."

"No, Miss Vallie. I believe you could fill the role very nicely. Of course, if you have other obligations, I will understand."

Why did this make me feel guilty? I knew Mother would say it would be my Christian duty. Reverend Stephens would know I had no other obligations on Sundays. Ministers are like shepherds; they have a way of knowing what was going on with their flock.

I looked down at my toes and pretended to pick a piece of lint off my skirt before I glanced up at him. Then I heard myself say, "If it's only for a month, I can do it."

His face broke into a wide grin, which gave him that younger look I had seen the other day. "Thank you. A burden has been lifted from my shoulders. I will help in any way I can. If it is convenient for you, I will stop by your house tomorrow evening with lesson plans."

"That will be fine. I know Mother will want you to stay for dinner." Mother always liked to cook for guests, and having the minister as a guest would make her doubly pleased.

Including Lucy and Davey, I knew there were only seven children in that Sunday class, and I knew all of them. I also knew little Danny Hobbs was a handful and Patsy Perkins a spoiled brat, but I told myself I could suffer through one month. It seemed I was getting good at piling one aggravation on top of another.

Chapter 38

Monday was my day to work at Lockwood. I hoped the atmosphere in the big house had improved since that incident of Peg showering Miss Gilbert with a plate of food.

I was determined to show my Channing Fox letter to Miss Adelaide so she could consult Mr. Alex. With Peg and Miss Gilbert at odds, I didn't want to burden Miss Adelaide further, but I did need to know how to respond to Mr. Fox, or if I should just forget the letter altogether.

Peg met me at the door, but without the cheery welcome I was used to. She was all business. My first duty was to take the breakfast tray up to Miss Gilbert, which I did.

The prim and proper nanny accepted it without so much as a thank you. She said, "When I am finished, I'll ring the bell for you."

Certainly she would because she always rang the bell when she wanted something. Perhaps that was what needled Peg. Her equal in the house ringing a bell to be waited on and then complaining. I didn't blame Peg, but she should have talked with Miss Adelaide.

As I went about my duties of the day, it wasn't until it was time to leave that I found Miss Adelaide in the office. To my chagrin, Mr. Alex was there also. He always made me nervous for no obvious reason. The thought passed in my mind that I should forget the whole thing and throw Channing Fox's letter away. It was a fleeting thought because I found myself standing before my employers and saying, "Please excuse me, but I have a problem and I need your advice."

They were both seated at the desk and looked up in surprise.

"What is it, Vallie?" asked Miss Adelaide. "If it is about the disagreeable situation between Peg and Miss Gilbert, we are in the process of finding a replacement for Miss Gilbert."

Aside from that good news, I still felt uncomfortable. "No ma'am." I pulled the letter from my apron pocket. "It's this letter I received. My parents thought I should ask you about it." I handed her the letter.

Adelaide read it and handed it to her husband. "This looks like something you should handle," she said.

I stood there feeling like a dunce.

"Interesting," Alex said. "I would like to see it more in business form. Do you know Mr. Fox?" he asked me.

"No, sir," I replied and then went on to explain about Miss Eva and my sketches.

"Are you interested in pursuing this?" Mr. Alex asked. "If the man is sincere this may be a good opportunity for you."

"He did send me a check for the two sketches he wanted to use," I said.

Mr. Alex offered a kind smile and handed the letter back to me. "Then, I believe you should meet with Mr. Fox. If he offers a contract, I will be pleased to go over it with you."

Adelaide clapped her hands together. "Oh, Vallie. Lottie always said you have a talent with your clothing ideas, and to be able to put them onto paper is a special gift. This is exciting!"

I think Miss Addie was more excited than I was. The thought of going to Washington to meet with Channing Fox and somehow getting caught up in the business world scared me to death.

When I got home, I told my parents what had transpired. They agreed that I should respond to Mr. Fox and arrange for a meeting.

That same evening, Reverend Stephens came by to have supper and go over lesson plans. He and I went out to the back porch and sat at the table where I did a lot of my sketching. One of them was on the table. Before I could pick it up, Wendell Stephens was eyeing it. He said, "This is very good. Who is the artist?"

I had never been called an artist. "It's something I do in my spare time," I replied, with a hint of embarrassment.

He smiled. "I like to paint, although I get little free time."

I put the sketch in the drawer and he pulled out papers from a valise he carried. "Now, Miss Vallie, you will find these lessons easy as they are all bible stories. Miss Stratton prepared them to go along with the scripture of the day."

"I am a bit nervous about this, Mr. Stephens. I know the lesson is only for a half hour, but there are a couple of children who may take it in their heads to run out onto the altar or get into some kind of mischief." I thought it best to let him know my concerns.

He thought for a few seconds. "There isn't a way of cordoning off that back area of the chapel, but I don't believe that has been a problem for Miss Stratton."

Knowing Miss Stratton, I believe all she had to do was glower at the kids and they were afraid to leave their seats.

"I'll tell you what. The parents usually wait for the children and it's a time I can be with a small group to solve any concerns with the chapel itself. It seems there are always some maintenance or lack of funding issues that need to be addressed. I'll make it a point to check in during your lesson."

"Thank you. I'm most likely worrying for no reason, but sometimes I'm good at that. But you know, children lose their attention after a few minutes. Just like those of us who are older, after listening for about ten minutes we're ready to move on." I hoped he would pick up on the subtle hint.

He chuckled. "Are you saying my sermons are too lengthy?"

I felt my face burn. "I guess I did mean that."

He nodded his head. "I stand up there and I can hear all the fidgeting going on, but it is so important to get the message across. One idea leads to another. Believe it or not, I was warned about that in divinity school." He let his eyes wander to the back yard where evening shadows were spreading. "I look around and see the wonder of our world and I don't want people to forget it is the Lord's doing."

We both sat silent for a minute before he said, "I'll go to my little place and write my sermon for Sunday." He shrugged, "I do that anyway, but then I don't stick to it."

I couldn't help but laugh. "Do you know you are quite different than when you're the preacher?"

"In what way?" he asked.

"Do you want me to be honest?"

"That would help," he said.

I wanted to get my words straight before I replied, "Well, for one thing when you're the preacher, you seem stiff and unbending. When you're not the minister, you're relaxed and comfortable to be around."

He thought about it. "That's honest enough. I do have to keep my place as the preacher."

"You will always have the respect due a minister, but I think people would like to see more of the true Wendell Stephens as I have." Why was I talking to this man like this?

I apologized. "I'm sorry, I guess I got carried away."

He shook his head. "There is no need to apologize. You have told me something I already know. I'll work on it, if you'll promise to not worry about teaching Sunday school."

That brought a smile to my face. "We both have something to work on."

He handed me the small bundle of lesson plans. "I shall see you on Sunday," he said.

We went back into the kitchen where Mother and Nora were finishing cleaning up.

He walked over to Mother. "Mrs. Brown, I thank you for a lovely meal, and for lending your daughter in Miss Stratton's place."

Those words pleased Mother. "We are happy to have you as a guest any time," she said.

"With a delicious meal like the one I had, I may take you up on that offer. Good evening, ladies," he said and went out the door.

Mother shook her head. "It's such a shame he doesn't have a wife to look after him."

I smiled to myself. Mother was always one to be concerned for others. The Reverend Stephens seemed to be satisfied with his life just the way it was.

Chapter 39

On Wednesday, Nora and I finished the laundry by the afternoon. She went to help Mother in the kitchen, and I decided to skip out on the work and take a ride to Tizzie Nelson's old place. I hoped Miss Fannie would be there and I wasn't disappointed.

She was sitting on the porch in a rocker and nursing the baby.

"Well, Miss Vallie," Miss Fannie called. "It's nice to see you. Put your horse by the shed. There's fresh water in the troth."

I rode Ches to the shed near the house and unsaddled him. It was a hot August day but there was a slight breeze and a small scrub tree where I could tether him and give him some shade. "I won't be long, Ches," I told him. Then I walked to where Fannie sat.

"There's cold tea in the ice box," she said. "Go in and pour yourself a glass and bring one out for me."

"I didn't know you had an ice box," I said.

"Jess had it delivered a couple of days ago. He wants to move over here as soon as we can."

"Miss Addie and Miss Lottie will be sad to see you leave Lockwood," I told her.

Fannie smiled at me. Her red hair had streaks of gold from the summer sun. "It will be a change for all of us, but, Vallie, life is always changing and we have to learn to change with it."

I went into the house to get the tea thinking about what she had just said. Life is always changing. I had come to talk with her about my dilemma with Channing Fox. Her words were like an omen from above.

I chipped some ice with the ice pick before I filled two glasses with the cold tea and took them out to the porch. She had finished nursing and the baby lay contentedly in her arms. I placed the glass on a small wicker table that sat between two rockers and took my place across from her.

"I'll bet you and Mr. Jess sit out here and watch how Tizzie's place is changing," I said. "Do you think it will always be known as the Nelson place?"

Fannie chuckled. "Probably," she said. "Jess and I sit out here when we get a minute." She added, "Jess is getting pretty tired, but he's given his notice at Lockwood and we'll be your neighbors in a couple weeks."

"I'm happy for that," I said. Then I changed the subject. "Miss Fannie, I came to talk to you about a problem."

She looked quizzical. "A problem?"

I told her the whole story and she didn't answer right away, which made me wonder what she was thinking. Suddenly, she broke into a wide smile. "Vallie I think that is the best news I've heard in a while. Of course you should get a letter off to that Mr. Fox. I'd love to go to Washington. And, I know Addie, if she was excited it meant that she would go with you to be in the middle of things."

"She didn't say that," I said.

Fannie laughed. "No, but I know how her mind works. Wouldn't that be fun? You, me and Adelaide off to the big city for a few days?"

I knew my face took on a questionable look. "What about the babies?"

Fannie pursed her lips. "Ooh, I hadn't thought of that. I'm too used to doing as I please."

That was the first time I ever heard Miss Fannie make a thoughtless remark.

She offered a weak smile. "I guess I got carried away, Vallie. You should go ahead and meet with this man. It will either be a whole new way of life for you, or you will know instantly that it is not what you want to do. Give yourself the opportunity and you will never regret it."

I left Miss Fannie feeling much better. She was right. If I didn't follow through with this, I might have big regrets down the road. On my way home, Ash Corbin popped into my mind and I knew I wanted to tell him. I hadn't responded to his letter. Perhaps that was the way it should be, yet I knew that if I was in Washington again, I wanted to see him.

That evening after I finished the dishes and swept the wood floor, I went upstairs to the room I shared with Nora and pulled my private box from under my bed. I read Ash's letter once more, then

I penned a reply as well as sending an answer to Channing Fox. I knew Billy was coming over this evening to see Nora, and I knew he would take the letters into the Berryville post office for me.

Then the thought struck me that when Billy and Nora married, this room would be mine. I'd never had a room to myself. I had to wonder what it would be like, but I did like the thought of it.

Chapter 40

Billy Wood had mailed my letters because a week later I received a reply from both Ash and Channing Fox. Mr. Fox wanted me to come to Washington where he would explain what my duties would be and show me around his clothing facility. I read the short note with both anticipation and reticence. What would I be getting myself into? Could I mail him sketches or would it mean moving to the city?

On the other hand, if I did get hired, it would mean no more cleaning and helping at Lockwood, no more laundry for eight people, no more long-winded sermons or teaching Sunday school.

That wasn't fair to Reverend Stephens. I only had two more lessons before the regular teacher returned. And, Reverend Stephens had been a big help. The lessons were simple Bible stories, but he had dropped by to ask if I needed anything. He even taught the children a song with his soft mellow singing voice and the children were so happy to see him. Wendell Stephens was very different from the preacher on the altar.

As for Ash's letter, I waited until after dinner and I had read bedtime nursery rhymes to Lucy and Davey. I made fast work of the nursery rhymes as

213

I was eager to get into the privacy of my room to savor every word Ash had written.

September 13, 1924
My dear Val,

I cannot tell you how pleased I was to receive your reply to my first letter nor can I express my joy at the thought you might be coming to Washington.

Mr. Channing Fox is well known among the upper circles here in the city. The fact that he is interested in your designs is a feather in your cap as he would not have contacted you if he didn't think they were special. Miss Eva Lou deserves a big thank you.

I will not say if you come, I'll say when you come, I will meet you at the train and have a room reserved at a nearby hotel or make any other arrangements you need.

You have brightened my spirit and I have something to look forward to, so please don't disappoint me. This position I have gets more distasteful every day, but I keep my goal in mind and know it will only be until spring.

Please write as soon as you know your plan. I can't wait to see you again.

With my fondest regards,
Ash

After reading his letter, I knew what I was going to do. I was going to Washington.

When I told Mother and Father of my decision, they both agreed that I should pursue Mr. Fox's invitation. Then the stumbling blocks appeared. They forbid me to ride the train alone. Neither of the boys could go as they were needed on the farm. Mother couldn't go because she had too many responsibilities. Actually, that was good news because I couldn't imagine having Mother as a companion, especially if Ash was involved. And, Nora was needed to take some of the burden off Mother. For the short time we would be gone, I was sure Mother could make that one small sacrifice. After all, the hard work of summer was over. However, it was not my place to contradict my parents.

What enthusiasm I had built up was quickly torn down.

When Nora and Billy came in from their evening stroll, they could tell by the look on my face that I wasn't happy. Mother and Father were in the parlor.

"What's wrong Vallie?" Nora asked.

I told her in a matter of a few words. I added that Ash said he could meet me at the train station and make any arrangements I needed. In a voice my parents couldn't hear, I said, "I don't know how they expect me to meet with Mr. Fox if I can't go by myself and no one can go with me. Mr. Fox wants to meet with me next Friday."

Nora took my hand. "Oh, Vallie. There must be a way."

Billy had been thoughtful. "I don't see why you can't go," he said. "You and Nora could take a late train on Thursday and get an early train home on Saturday. If Ash is willing to guide you around, he would watch out for your welfare. It would be a good trip for Nora. I can take both of you to the Bluemont station and pick you up when you return."

I was liking Billy more and more. I hoped my parents would go along with his suggestion as this sounded like a great plan to me.

The three of us went into the parlor. When Billy proposed the idea to my parents, Father considered it silently, but Mother said no as neither one of us knew anything about the city. After a couple of quiet minutes, Father said, "I don't see any reason why they can't go. The boys are here and it's only for a day and a half."

"I don't think we should depend on Ashton to squire them around," Mother said.

"He's a reliable young man," countered Father. "I trust him or I wouldn't let them go."

Mother rolled her eyes and shook her head.

I was back to my former happy mood. I asked Billy if he was going into Berryville soon and if he would send two telegrams for me.

He was going Monday morning. By sending telegrams, Mr. Fox and Ash would have enough time to make any arrangements, so that my appearance in Washington wouldn't be unexpected.

With a light step on the stairs, I went to my room to jot off my messages telling Mr. Fox and Ash that Nora and I would arrive in Washington on the last train from Bluemont on Thursday evening.

I would tell Miss Adelaide on Monday that I wouldn't be available for the rest of the week.

I went to bed feeling a rosy glow. Was this going to be a turning point in my life?

Chapter 41

When I told Miss Adelaide the reason I wouldn't be at Lockwood on Thursday, she was happy for me. "You must tell me all about it when you return," she had said. I wondered if I would have the courage she had shown when she went to Washington to work during the war. She was by herself until she met Miss Fannie at a boarding house. Boarding house. I'm not sure I liked the sound of that.

Nora and I packed an overnight tote bag. We would wear the same garments we wore on the train. We took a nightgown, toothbrush, and hairbrush. Nora brought a small vial of perfume Billy had given to her and said we could share it. Miss Fannie said the hotel would have soap and towels.

Billy came to the house at four o'clock Thursday afternoon. Our train was scheduled to leave at five-fifteen. It was another round of hugs and goodbyes before we climbed into the red, still shiny farm truck. Billy took good care of his prized vehicle.

Mother looked anxious. She wasn't sold on Nora and me going to the city. She insisted we carry an umbrella. "It might rain," she said. "And, you can use it as a weapon if you have to." Father tried to hide his smile.

218

We were two of the five passengers who boarded the train in Bluemont, but as we stopped at the stations across the mountain our train car was full as were most of the others.

I didn't let Nora know I held any reservations, but, although Billy had sent the telegrams, I wasn't sure they were received by Ash and Mr. Fox. They could have been intervened when they were delivered. What if Ash didn't meet us at the train station? It would be dark when we arrived. What if there were no taxis? What if there were no hotel rooms available? All these doubts hit me the closer we got to Washington, and I could feel my palms getting sweaty under my brown cotton gloves. I was glad I hadn't worn white or they would be stained.

As the train slowed and pulled into the station, Nora looked over at me with a tentative smile. "Well, here we are, Vallie."

I nodded and tried to look confident. I couldn't fool my sister.

"Let's look at it as an adventure and see if our parents raised two resourceful young ladies," she remarked, and I had to chuckle.

We picked up our tote bags and purses and followed the line of passengers departing the train car.

"You ladies enjoy the city while you're here," said the conductor as he helped us down the steel steps onto the platform. We gravitated toward a bench as I scanned the crowd for any sign of Ash. He wasn't in sight.

Union Station was cavernous, noisy and full of people. What if Ash couldn't find us? Try as I might negative thoughts still arose.

Nora sat on the bench, but I remained on my feet craning my neck.

"Vallie, come and sit down. If Ashton doesn't show up, we'll ask someone to hail a taxi for us and go to the nearest hotel," Nora said.

"How can you be so calm?" I asked.

She smiled, "Because Billy told me what to do if our plans didn't work out."

I felt myself beginning to relax. "Billy is one surprise after another," I said as I took a seat next to her.

"He is that," she agreed. "We'll sit here for a few minutes. It could be Ash is delayed."

I was glad Nora had come with me. Since she had become engaged to Billy Wood, she had become more self-assured. She now took her rightful place as the older sister.

"Val!" I heard a voice call and watched as Ashton Corbin came hurrying in our direction. He was dressed in a yellow sweater, tan wool pants and a driver's cap. With a wide smile on his pleasant face, I knew he was as happy to see me as I was to see him.

"I'm sorry I'm late," he apologized. "I had to finish up some work before I take tomorrow off."

That was welcome news. Any anxious moments I had spent, were completely washed away now that Ash was here.

"Hi, Nora. It's nice to see you," he said as he doffed his cap in her direction. "Do you have any cases for me to carry?"

We shook our heads. "We traveled as light as we could," I said.

"Are you hungry? I've reserved a room at the George Washington Hotel for you. We can get a bite to eat near there, if you'd like," he said.

We had shared a ham sandwich on the train and I was starved. I hoped Nora felt the same. I looked at her and she nodded. "We'd like," I said to Ash.

He had driven his coupe. Although it was a bit crowded in the front seat, I didn't mind sitting shoulder to shoulder with Ash. He looked over at me and smiled as he started the car. Although it was getting dark, the street lights helped. Nora sat quietly watching the city pass on our way to the hotel.

The eating place was a small restaurant with a lot to offer. Ash had a fried chicken dinner, Nora had a hot roast beef sandwich, and I spied fish and chips on the menu. I wanted to tell Miss Fannie that I had fish and chips just like she told me to, so Ash ordered them for me.

"The best ones are in the Irish pubs," Ash said. "But, Mr. O'Brien owns this place so they might be just as good."

The three of us ate our meals as though we hadn't eaten in a week. That was not only because we were hungry, but because the food was so delicious. Nora looked at Ash. "Your Mr. O'Brien is a wonderful cook, I'd like to have his recipes."

"He says they're his secrets," Ash answered. "But, he may trade a couple in exchange for your dessert recipes."

Nora blushed at the compliment and I could see she was pleased. "I guess those are my secrets," she said. After our late dinner, we walked the half block to the hotel. When we reached it, both Nora and I were in awe. It was a massive red building six or seven stories high. The street level held various shops, even a theater.

Ash escorted us into the lobby and seated us in two plush chairs before he went to the receiving desk. He came back with a key. "The bell hop will be here shortly," he said. "What time is your appointment with Mr. Fox?"

"Nine o'clock," I answered.

"I'll be here at seven-thirty. We can have breakfast and then I will take you to his place. It's only a few blocks from here."

The bell hop arrived, Ash handed him our key. "Sleep well, ladies," Ash said. He watched as we followed the guide to the elevator. I turned and looked back at Ash. He held a smile and waved before the elevator operator closed the door, and we were carried away to the fourth floor.

Inside the room, I handed the bell hop a dime and he left us to be overwhelmed by our whole day. Nora went into the bathroom and exclaimed, "Indoor plumbing and a bath tub!" Then she came out, pulled the long brocade drape aside, and peered down at the city below. Billy was right. He said I should take in all the city has to offer while

I'm here. "It's like looking through the pages of a magazine. Vallie, I'm just going to climb into my nightgown and go to bed. Maybe that will make me feel normal. I get the right side of this bed."

I laughed. Never had I seen Nora so excited. "I think we're in fantasy land," I said. "Do you think we're going to wake up and find it's all a dream?"

Chapter 42

It wasn't a dream. Nora and I were up at six o'clock. The first thing she did was go to the window and open the long drapes. "Oh, Vallie, the city is waking up. I see a trolley and all sorts of delivery trucks, horses, buggies, wagons, and workers going to their shops."

She turned and looked at me. I was still lying in bed trying not to think about my meeting with Channing Fox. "Do you think you could live here, Vallie?"

"Why do you ask?"

"Because I have a feeling that if Mr. Fox wants you to work for him, you are going to have to move here." She turned back to the window not waiting for an answer. "If you lived here, Billy and I could come and visit."

Nora's mind was working overtime. Mine was clouded with the meeting that might seal or doom my future, and dreading how much this trip was going to cost. I would settle up with Ash before we left. I said, "We'd better start getting ready to meet Ash downstairs."

"Yes, we should," Nora replied. "I'm not fond of elevators. They're too noisy and shaky. They make my knees wobbly. There must be stairs."

I wrinkled my nose at her. "Walk four flights of stairs?"

"Why not? It will be good exercise after that long train ride," she reasoned.

The hotel not only furnished washcloths, towels and soap, there was also rose-scented toilet water. Nora and I both took a sponge bath to feel clean from the smoky smell and grime of the train car. We vowed we would take the very back seat in the passenger car on the way back home. That way a cigar smoker couldn't sit behind us.

I sniffed my tan, long-sleeved cotton dress and undergarments to discern if it smelled of smoke. The smell was faint, and I hoped it would disappear by the time I met with Mr. Fox. Or, perhaps the perfume would cover the scent.

Nora was dressed in a plaid dress with a square neck, whereas mine was V-neck. We both wore a cross necklace that Mother had insisted we bring. I guess that was to show we were Christian women and to keep the male opportunists away.

Mother didn't have anything to worry about after we saw the daring dress of the Washington set. We did wear the modern cloche hats made of felt that complemented our plain dresses. Leaving the umbrella behind and donning our gloves, we picked up our pocket books, shawls and the room key. We were ready to meet Ash and whatever Washington held in store for us; two young women from a small county about seventy miles west, just over the Blue Ridge Mountains.

We walked down the four flights of stairs. I looked at Nora. "When we get back, you can take these stairs if you want to, but I'm taking the elevator."

Nora shrugged.

Ash was waiting in the opulent lobby as he said he would. He looked cleanly shaven, nattily dressed, and full of life. "You ladies look fresh and bright for a day on the town."

I couldn't help but smile because I was happy to see him. "I don't know how ready we are," I replied.

"It's going to be a great day because you're both here," he said. "Once you get your meeting over, we're going to take in the sights that Washington has to offer. I hope you are wearing your walking shoes."

"They're the only shoes we brought because we weren't sure how much walking we would have to do," said Nora.

"We'll go to O'Brien's for breakfast and then I'll drive you to the Fox place. Nora, will you be accompanying Val or will I have the pleasure of your company while she's getting the low down from Channing Fox?"

"There's safety in numbers." I said. "I feel so tense Nora is coming with me so she can remember what I may forget."

Ash gently pressed my arm. "You're going to do just fine, Val."

The doorman opened the door for us as we exited to the street. There was a slight fog that Ash said would become a clear fall day. He said that wasn't unusual for Washington because of the rivers. I don't think Nora cared any more than I did. We were looking forward to a morning that didn't start with our usual farm chores.

Mr. O'Brien's cozy restaurant was packed with customers. Ash found a place for the three of us in a small room off the back. We sat in a tight booth and once again Ash and my shoulders were touching. The closeness sent a ripple of pleasure through me.

Mr. Fox's business was a few blocks away, and we elected to walk thinking it would help both Nora and me to relax. Ash escorted us and said he would be waiting in his car when we were through. He thought it would be about two hours. If we didn't see his coupe parked on the street, we were to wait until he showed up.

Nora and I stood in front of a three story, red brick building with a sign above the entry that read, Fox Fashions. On each side of the entryway that led up to the front door there were two large display windows with mannequins depicting dresses for tea, evening wear and a shiny, shimmy dress for dancing. The mannequin wearing the dancing dress also was adorned with two long strands of pearls and a fancy headband. We were in awe.

Nora looked at me. "Can you imagine show-ing up at a barn dance dressed like that?"

We laughed aloud. That little aside was enough that any anxieties I held flew away. We walked up to the wood door that held a small window. It was locked but opened within a few seconds.

A gentleman dressed in a suit, white shirt and tie stood there and said, "Good morning, ladies."

I introduced myself and Nora.

"Come right in. Mr. Fox is expecting you. The store opens at nine and you're right on time. Please follow me and I'll take you to his office."

The young man didn't introduce himself, but there was nothing for us to do except follow him to wherever he was leading.

We went up a flight of steps into a reception area where a lady sat at a secretary desk with a typewriter on a stand next to her. A tall wood file cabinet was in a corner. She looked up when the door opened.

"Good morning JC," she said to the young man.

"Good morning, this is Miss Brown and her sister. I believe Mr. Fox is expecting them."

"Yes, he is. Welcome young ladies," she said and offered a slight smile. Her brown hair was neatly arranged in a French twist. She was trim and wore a white blouse and black skirt. Observing the neatness of her office space, she was the picture of efficiency. She rose from her chair, walked to a door, opened it without a knock and we heard her say, "Miss Brown and her sister are here."

The one she called JC leaned down to Nora and me and in a low voice said, "That's my mother. She'll probably congratulate me for getting to work on time. And, don't let the old man rattle you, he's my father."

I tried not to show my surprise and I'm sure Nora did the same although I didn't look over at her.

The secretary returned and showed us into the office of Mr. Fox. He stood from behind his desk, a man of average height with hair color that is slow to show the streaks of gray creeping in. His brown eyes peered over the spectacles he wore. Without a smile or word of greeting, he stood as if inspecting both Nora and me before he offered, "Have a chair young ladies. Which one of you is Vallie May?"

I felt as reticent as I did when I had to talk to Mr. Lockwood. However, I was here with a purpose so I gathered myself together and said, "I'm Vallie and this is my sister, Nora." Nora nodded to him and he offered a wan smile.

"We'll get right to business. Miss Brown, may I call you Vallie?"

"Yes, you may. I'd feel more comfortable."

"Well, I certainly want you to feel comfortable. Now, Miss Vallie, I am very interested in seeing further of your work. Miss Eva says that you sketch when you have free time. Is that right?"

I nodded and reached into my pocketbook and pulled out some sketches I had done. "I brought a few in case you would like to see them."

He took the folded papers and smoothed them out on his desk. "Where did you learn to do this?"

I shrugged. "I just looked at pictures in magazines and drew what pleased me."

Then he looked up with a wide smile. "So you have a natural talent. I had to send my son to school to learn how to design. I will offer you a position here at Fox Fashions at a salary of seventy-five cents an hour. Your work hours would be from eight in the morning to five in the afternoon, an hour for lunch, and your weekends would be free, unless we have pressing work. I don't expect an answer today. Now, I'll show you and your sister our work place."

Channing Fox was dressed in a white shirt with rolled up sleeves, a plaid brown tie and brown pants. His shoes were shined. I assume if an important customer showed up all he had to do was don his suit jacket.

I glanced at Nora and raised an eyebrow. I wasn't sure what to make of Channing Fox. I never expected to earn seventy-five cents an hour. At least, I didn't fall off the chair when he said it. I had worked for a dollar a day for Miss Tizzie.

There was nothing for Nora and me to do except follow him as he led us through the outer office and down the flight of stairs. The stairs were separated from his shop and showroom by a door. We walked through a corridor with offices on either side. The office doors had names etched into the opaque glass. He didn't open any of them, but I did see the words Carl Rich, Accountant on one and James Gray, Records on another.

At the end of the corridor, Mr. Fox opened another door and Nora and I walked out to a stair landing. The view almost took my breath away. From that vantage point we could see the whole factory. In one area, four rows of women sat at sewing machines. To the left were stacks of material on shelves and beyond were large crates and boxes. Mr. Fox led us down the flight of stairs and began the tour. This place was noisy with the rat-tat-tat of sewing machines, workers hauling carts and shouting to each other to be heard over the din.

I noticed four men dressed in tan shirts and trousers who didn't seem to be working. Mr. Fox explained they were floor supervisors for the different work stations. "You see," he said, "we have designers, pattern makers, seamstresses, tailors, material handlers, and warehouse workers. Time is money and everyone has to be paid."

By the time he finished I was speechless. I looked at Nora and the expression on her face told me she was as wordless as I was. We followed Mr. Fox up the stairs, where we stopped on the landing and took one last look at the place that had seemed to be in another world.

We were back in the corridor. "The design offices are here," he explained. "I feel they need a quiet work area. This is where you will work, Vallie." Mr. Fox opened the door, and inside at a lovely walnut desk, sat JC Fox.

He looked up with a bright smile, rose from his chair and came around the desk to greet us. "Welcome, young ladies. You brighten my work space."

"I understand you've met my son, JC," Mr. Fox said to us. "He's not as dangerous as he appears." Then to JC he said, "Your mother tells me you managed to get to work on time for a change."

I wasn't sure what to make of this exchange between father and son, but I found it refreshing after being overwhelmed by the factory scene.

"Our last stop is the shop where they can see our fashions and dressing and fitting rooms. You can come with us if you'd like," Mr. Fox said.

"If you're not going to deduct the time from my meager wage, Dad."

Mr. Fox tapped him on the shoulder. "You're worth every penny."

JC laughed. "It's close to lunch time. Once we've finished with the most attractive spot in this place, how would you young ladies like to go to a free lunch?"

I shook my head and smiled at this young man who wasn't too much older than we were. "We have someone waiting for us once we're through," I said.

"We do thank you for the offer," Nora replied. I think they were the first words she had uttered since we had entered Fox Fashions.

"Too bad," said JC. "You'll be missing a great opportunity."

A half smile appeared and Channing Fox shook his head. "Not much of one," he said to Nora and me.

Feeling light hearted and more relaxed, the four of us toured the lavish shop. Both Nora and I admired the fine materials and fashionable clothing on display.

"Our customers expect the best and that's what we are here to provide," said Mr. Fox. "If you decide to come and work with us Miss Vallie, you will be dressing the important ladies of Washington."

He picked up a large envelope and handed it to me. "All the information is in here. I thank you and Miss Nora for coming, and I will expect an answer by next Friday."

My mind was befuddled with all that I had seen. All I could say was, "Thank you, sir. I promise you will have an answer by then."

JC looked out the window and saw Ash was standing beside his car. "Is that Ash Corbin waiting for you?"

I nodded. "Yes. He's been good enough to help us navigate Washingon."

"I haven't seen him all summer," he said. "Hey, Dad. I'm going to take an early lunch and I'll work an hour of overtime."

Channing Fox gave his son a wary eye. "I'll make an exception for today."

We said our goodbyes and the three of us crossed the street to where Ashton Corbin stood with a slight frown. I wasn't sure he was all that pleased to see us coming accompanied by JC Fox.

Chapter 43

The restaurant chosen was unimposing on the outside, much like many of the commercial buildings in Washington, but once we stepped inside we were surprised to see a large dining room with a windowed wall overlooking the Potomac. The calm and peaceful river glistened in the sunlight. I looked at Nora and she raised an eyebrow.

The host dressed in a black suit, white shirt and black tie, checked his reservation list. "Of course, Mr. Fox. Your mother called and said to reserve one of our finest tables for four. Please follow me."

Ash had been rather quiet on our trip here even though it was obvious he was well acquainted with JC. I had gathered from the conversation that they were both part of a regular group of partygoers. JC said he wondered why Ash hadn't been around for most of the summer. It was also obvious from JC's comments that Ash was a hit among the young ladies, which seemed to make Ash uncomfortable.

Mother's admonition, "Don't get too close" came to the forefront of my brain. I glanced across the table to Nora. Their heads close together, she was in quiet conversation with JC. Nora, my quiet sister, talking up a storm. I found that odd although Nora was one to make others feel comfortable.

Shouldn't that be the other way around? After all, it was JC who had set this up. I felt the setting was a bit stiff, however, Nora seemed to take it in stride.

No one seemed to take note of our attire, which fit fine in Mr. O'Brien's cozy eatery, but it felt common among the linen tablecloths, fine china, crystal water glasses and silver utensils. JC was smiling at Nora and she was smiling back. Didn't JC notice the engagement ring on Nora's finger? Had Nora forgotten that she and Billy Wood were engaged? I found JC Fox a little too sure of himself. Nora seemed to find him most entertaining.

Ash sat to my right. He seemed to sense my consternation. "The Chesapeake crab soup is very good here," he said.

His words broke my reverie and I gave him a thankful smile. "I've never had crab soup," I replied.

That statement got JC's attention. "Never had crab soup?"

Nora said, "JC, the only crabs we have over the mountain are crawdads. I'll bet you've never had turtle soup."

He snickered. "Can't say as I have. It must be a day's work getting the turtle out of his shell. What do you say, Nora? Are you up to trying a cup of crab soup? It's rich."

"I wouldn't expect anything else in this place," she said, and they both actually giggled.

I looked over at Ash. He was not amused. This was not the Nora I knew, and I had to wonder if the air in Washington had gone to her head.

The waiter appeared in black trousers, white shirt, black vest and bow tie. "Would you care to see our specialty beverage list?" he asked.

"We'll take your most popular toasting drink," said JC. "We have newfound friends to salute."

The waiter was gone in a flash and returned with a bottle and four flute glasses. He showed the label to JC and then proceeded to open the pale and bubbly beverage, which brought a gasp from Nora when the cork popped. Her hands flew to her mouth to cover the noise causing her and JC to giggle again.

"Since the government outlawed alcohol, enterprising people have done their best to mimic it," JC explained.

I thought of the time Ash had taken me and Jake to the ball game, and he had bought beer at a little spot near the ball park. Apparently, there were still places to get illegal hooch if you knew the right spot or maybe where the policemen turned their heads. And, I knew that over the mountain people knew how to make their own wine, beer and hard cider.

The waiter never lost his poise. He poured and served the bubbly mixture before he turned and left.

I glanced sideways under hooded brows to see if our table had attracted the attention of other diners because I was beginning to feel embarrassed. I thought Nora was acting like a school girl, but Joseph Channing Fox seemed to be enjoying himself.

Nora had asked him what the initials JC stood for and he had told us Joseph Channing, saying his mother refused to name him Channing.

"Why don't they call you Joe or Joseph?" Nora had asked.

"Because JC sounds more important," he had replied, and they had both snickered like it was a well-kept secret.

JC raised his flute. "To our lovely young ladies."

Nora did the same and said, "And, to these Washington gentlemen."

My quiet sister had confounded me from the minute we stepped into this restaurant. However, I was determined not to let my confusion show, so I clinked my flute with the other three. What did Nora and I know about a toast except what we'd seen in the movies? If she was putting on an act, she was doing a fine job.

The waiter had taken our lunch order. We all had a cup of Chesapeake crab soup followed by a silver tray of fancy delicate sandwiches, which we passed around. I wasn't sure what I was eating, but they were delicious. After the soup and sandwiches, the waiter brought a dessert cart filled with all sorts of pastries. Everything looked so tempting, it was difficult to decide on one. I settled for a chocolate torte topped with whipped cream and a raspberry. Nora chose a cream puff.

"JC, Nora bakes the tastiest desserts," Ash said as he looked up from his plate of French apple pie.

Nora blushed at the impromptu compliment.

JC smiled at her. "That doesn't surprise me. I'm sure you have many talents. I'd like to taste one of your creations."

"Any time you care to venture over the mountain, I promise I'll make something special," she replied.

I thought my sister was openly flirting with Joseph Channing Fox and the sooner we left this restaurant, the more I liked that idea. JC would be returning to work. Ash, Nora and I could get on with our day of seeing what sites in Washington time allowed.

We piled into Ash's car with he, Nora and I in the front and JC merrily enjoying the rumble seat. Ash drove to Fox Fashions where JC was to return to work. The thought crossed my mind that the carefree JC might change his mind. So, I discreetly touched the cross I wore and said a silent prayer.

When we reached the shop, JC hopped out of the seat and Ash got out of the car. They shook hands. "It was good to meet up with you," Ash said. "Thank your father for paying the tab." I wondered how sincere that statement was as I wasn't sure Ash had found the luncheon pleasant.

Then JC said, "How about you and I, Vallie and Nora taking in a cinema tonight? *The Sea Hawk* is playing and gets good reviews in the *Post.*"

The windows of the coupe were rolled down allowing us to hear the conversation.

Ash hesitated. "The girls have an early train to catch, so I'm not sure…"

"Of course we would," I heard Nora say so Ash and JC could hear. I jabbed her in the ribs and whispered, "What's got into you? Have you forgotten you're engaged to marry Billy?"

She whispered back, "Certainly I haven't. This is my fling, Vallie. JC Fox just likes to have a good time. Haven't you seen he isn't serious about anything?"

I shook my head. "You call me the dreamer. What do you think Billy is going to say?"

"I'm going to tell him that JC is a friend of Ash and the four of us had a lovely lunch and went to the cinema. And, as JC is the son of the man you may end up working for, we couldn't afford to turn down his invitations."

"I don't think Billy is going to swallow that weak explanation," I countered.

Nora nodded her head. "Yes, he will as long as you don't tell him I acted like a flirtatious fool."

I gave her a disgusted look. "At least you recognize it."

Chapter 44

The Sea Hawk was an exciting moving picture about a galley slave who became a pirate. More exciting was the fact that Ash held my hand during the movie. The theater was dark so I don't think Nora noticed.

After we left the theater JC and Ash walked us to the hotel. Nora declined JC's invitation to go for a sandwich. "I've had a long wonderful day and I want to snare the bathtub before Vallie gets the chance. Thanks to both of you for making this a perfect time away from the cares of the day," she said.

"And, thank you for brightening my day," JC replied.

Ash said he would be here at seven-thirty to see that we made the early train. Nora and I headed toward the elevators as we turned and waved goodbye.

*****

This morning Nora is up before me and I am lying here on the bed remembering the warm feeling of Ash's hand in mine. In the afternoon he had taken us by all the notable buildings and statues in Washington. I had seen most of them when Luke and I were here, but I could view them a hundred

240

times and never tire of their majesty. Just to be with Ashton Corbin satisfied my day.

"Are you awake, Vallie?" Nora called from the bathroom that was just large enough to hold a sink, stool, and claw-foot bath tub.

"Yes. I'm just enjoying this comfortable bed."

She came into the bedroom. "You had better get dressed. We don't want to miss the train."

"Don't we? There will be plenty to do when we get home," I replied.

Nora was busy packing her tote, but stopped and looked at me. "I guess if you lived here, all you would have to do is get yourself ready for a day at Fox Fashions. Have you been thinking about it?"

I yawned as I forced myself out of bed and picked up my undergarments. "I haven't had time. This has been a whirlwind of activity. I'm tired."

"So am I, but Ash will be waiting, and I'm looking forward to getting home to see Billy."

I got up and sat on the edge of the bed. "I thought maybe JC had changed your mind. You certainly seemed to enjoy his company."

Nora nodded. "I did. He is just a big kid having a good time. Billy is my one and only."

"Well, that's good to hear. Mother would probably swoon and take to the bed if you broke your engagement." I was tying my shoes. "Of course, she was always big on Harold. Maybe the creep would start coming around again."

Nora wrinkled her nose at me. "Pack up your stuff and let's go meet Ash."

We took the stairs again, although last night I used the elevator and Nora chose to walk up. When we reached the lobby, Ash was waiting and he looked handsome dressed in his business three-piece suit and carrying a black fedora and an umbrella.

His smile was warm. "You may need that umbrella your Mother insisted you bring. The sky promises rain. It hasn't hit yet. With luck we'll make Union Station before the downpour."

For the last time on this trip we climbed into Ash's sporty coupe. For the last time on this trip, I would sit next to Ashton Corbin with our shoulders touching. I wondered if it would be the last time.

Ash escorted us to the train leaving for Bluemont station where Luke would be waiting in the buggy to drive us home. Nora boarded first, and as I prepared to mount the metal step Ash handed me a small wrapped package. "This is for you, Vallie."

I was without words so I impulsively leaned and kissed his cheek before I went up the three steps into the railcar. The conductor was standing right there and I saw him smile as I took my embarrassed self to our seat.

"Your face is flushed," Nora said. "Do you feel all right?"

I shook my head. "I don't know how I feel."

We rode the whole way to Bluemont without leaving the train at stop points. Both Nora and I were worn out and we slept most of the way as rain poured down. I had forgotten that Billy Wood said he would meet us at the station, but he was waiting with his prized red farm truck. The rain had turned to a gloomy mist.

Billy greeted Nora with a kiss as they walked to the vehicle. I had held back, feeling like this was a time for just the two of them. I fingered the little present Ash had given me. To know he held it, gave me pleasure and I didn't even care what was in that package.

It was around noon when we arrived home where Mother had a big pot of stew ready for lunch. She had also baked bread and apple cobbler. The kitchen was warm and the aroma of fresh baked bread made it warmer still. I was back home.

Tomorrow would be another service at Stone's Chapel and my fourth Sunday school lesson. I didn't look forward to it, but I could suffer through. If Reverend Stephens was working on shortening his sermons, it wasn't noticeable.

Uppermost on my mind was the small package Ash had given me.

While Nora was saying good night to Billy, I rushed up to the privacy of my room and pulled the present from my pocket. Inside was a silver disk, the size of a half-dollar. Imbedded in the center was a gold horseshoe and a note: Val, this is to bring you luck. Fond regards, Ash.

I clutched the charm in the palm of my hand, the same gift Ash had held in his. I could still feel the comforting warmth of his hand when we sat in the theater. I promised myself that I would carry it always.

Chapter 45

The next morning was like our usual Sunday mornings of hurry, hurry, hurry before we left for the service at Stone's Chapel. I was tired. In fact, I was so tired I thought I might nod off to sleep during Windy Wendell's sermon.

I could see Nora was as tired as I was, but we managed to complete our morning routine. Billy Wood picked her up for Sunday service now that they were engaged, and they sat in the pew in front of us. That gave the rest of us room to fidget if we felt the need. Billy always sat in that pew, and Nora being as slim as she was fit right in without squeezing the King family of four who sat with Billy. Of course no one owned the pews or reserved them. That was just the way it was.

The sermon was about the Prodigal son and how his father celebrated when he returned home. I thought that could be me running off to Washington to work for Channing Fox while Nora was left home with double the burden. I wonder how she would feel if I became the Prodigal daughter?

The thought quickly left my mind because Reverend Stephens only babbled on for ten minutes. I'm not sure I heard a word he said as my mind was occupied with the past couple days in Washington. I didn't even have a chance to look out the stained glass window next to me, which was alive with color from the morning sun.

After the service, I gathered the seven children and we went to the long narrow back room for the final lesson. I wasn't sure how I was going to make the lesson understood by four and five year olds, but I didn't have to worry. Wendell Stephens came to where we were collected, then he parted the room saying he was the Prodigal Son who had left. When he returned the children all rushed to him and clapped their hands. "You see," he said to them. "That's the way it was with the son's father. He was happy to have his son safe and back with his family."

When the thirty minutes were over, I dismissed the children to go with their parents. However, I wanted to stay and congratulate the minister on his sermon, even though I hadn't paid attention.

He smiled at me, which always gave him a younger and more relaxed appearance. "Well, Miss Vallie Brown, I took your sage advice and I have been working on it."

I know my face lit up like a Christmas tree from embarrassment. "That was unkind of me. I'm sorry."

"Don't be," he said. "It was for my own good." Then he changed the subject. "How was your trip to Washington? Will you be leaving us?"

I shook my head. "I don't know. It is such a big decision."

"I know it is," he said. "I was once in that kind of a spot, but I think I have chosen the right path."

This surprised me and raised my eyebrows. "You made a decision and you're not sure it was the right one?"

He paused for a moment. "It was the right decision at that time."

What did that mean? He didn't elaborate and I didn't ask.

Lucy ran in interrupting our conversation. "Father says it's time to leave," she said.

"If you feel the need to talk to someone, I'm available," said Reverend Stephens.

I thought it most unlikely that I would talk to him regarding my dilemma. It was a decision I had to make and I had less than a week to do it.

Sunday was our one day that we could do whatever we wanted. Once our big dinner was over in the early afternoon, we did as we pleased and ate sandwiches or popped popcorn for our evening meal.

Nora chose to spend the time with Billy and they went away in his farm truck. I went onto the back porch and pulled all of my sketches from the drawer where I kept them. I put them in a valise that Miss Fannie had found in the attic at Miss Tizzie's. She had no need for it and wondered if I would like it to keep my sketches in. The valise was brown leather, quite scratched up, and the corners were worn, but Father said rubbing in saddle soap would perk it up so it could be used. I had thrown it on the seat of an old chair we didn't use. Today, though, I decided to renew it as best I could. If I was going to work for Mr. Fox, I needed something to carry my drawings.

Luke came out onto the porch while I was shining up the leather.

"Vallie, is Ash going to try out for the Senators?"

I looked up at him. "I don't know. Why do you ask?"

"I'll be seventeen and finished with school this year, so I'd like to try out."

I didn't want to hurt his feelings, but I did want him to understand it was unlikely he could match up to big league pitchers. "Ash has had experience pitching in college and he's five years older than you. I'm sure experience counts."

"Ash said I'm good and I practice as much as I can."

"Ash said you would be a good college pitcher. He doesn't even know if he's good enough for the big league."

Luke let out a disgusted sigh. "Well, there's no way I can go to college, and I sure don't want to spend my life here as a farmer. Look at you, Vallie, you aren't cut out to be a farmer's wife. You've got the chance to do what you want to do and you can't make up your mind."

I shrugged. "It isn't that easy, Luke. It would be like turning my back on everything I know. It takes courage. I'm not sure I'm up to it."

"Shoot. You could go live with Miss Eva. She knows how to get around Washington and so does Ash. He likes you, Vallie."

And I like him, I thought. The possibility of living with Miss Eva never entered my mind. Perhaps that was something I could do until I was more settled. In some ways my teen-aged brother was more clever than I. Perhaps I could try it for a few months. I could always come back home.

Chapter 46

Two weeks later I was on the train to Washington. Billy and Nora took me up on the mountain to Bluemont station after tearful goodbyes from my family. Mark said he would take good care of my beloved Ches. I knew he would because he loved Ches almost as much as I did.

Mother said it was for her own selfish reasons she didn't want me to leave; Father said he guessed it was time for one bird to leave the nest; Lucy and Davey hadn't grasped the situation and wondered when I would be back; and Luke said he wished he could go with me. They all stood and waved while I fought back tears, especially when I saw Mother dabbing her eyes. My last glance was that of Ches contentedly grazing in the field.

It was a quiet ride to the station. My worldly possessions fit into two suitcases: one that belonged to our family and one borrowed from Billy.

Nora tried to ease my apprehension. "Ash is going to meet you at Union Station and drive you to Miss Eva's. Her letter said she is so pleased you will be staying with her. I'm sure she gets lonely."

"I wish I could be as pleased," I replied. "She's fussy. It is better than staying in a boarding house where I wouldn't know a soul. It will all be so different."

Billy surprised me by saying, "You'll do fine, Vallie. Of course it will be a whole new way of life, but give yourself a chance."

At the station, Billy handed my suitcases to the conductor. He was a tall man and looked very nice in his blue uniform and cap. "We have a good day for the trip," he said. "The trees are still in color. Miss you go ahead and take a seat, I'll see to your belongings."

I hugged Nora and Billy. "Thank you for driving me up."

"I'll write as often as I can," Nora said, "and I want to hear all about what you are doing in the big city."

I gave a weak smile as the conductor gave me a hand up the steel steps. I took a seat in the third row and next to the window where I could wave to my dear sister as the train left the station. I can't say as I felt any more at ease, and it reminded me of the saying in the Bible, "gird your loins". I gritted my teeth for whatever it was that lay ahead.

Ash was waiting on the platform when I stepped off the train. He came to me as quickly as he could get through the crowd and I burst into tears. He put his arm around my shoulders and whispered, "What's wrong, Val?"

I shook my head as I pulled my handkerchief from my pocket and started dabbing at the unwanted tearful display. What was wrong with me?

Ash picked up the suitcases and said, "Let's get out of here." I followed him to his sporty coupe.

I waited while he stashed my belongings in the rumble seat. He opened the door for me and made sure I was comfortably seated before he got into the driver's side. "Now, can you tell me the problem?"

I was down to a few sniffles. "I wish I knew."

"Is everything all right with your family?"

I nodded and tried to smile. "Everything is fine at home. I have been so anxious making this big change in my life, now that I have made the decision and am finally here, I think they were tears of relief."

He reached over and wiped an errant tear from my cheek. "I'm so glad you've come. I'll drop you by Miss Eva's to get settled and then I have to return to work. Let's go out for dinner so we can talk."

This time I gave him a wide smile. "You are good to me, Ash. I'm sorry for my weak moment."

"Don't be," he said. "It was a natural human reaction. Now that it's out of your system are you happy to be here?" he asked as he started the car and backed from the parking space.

I was delighted to be sitting next to Ashton Corbin. However, I would never tell him that. I said, "Yes, I am, and I thank you for meeting me at the station. Most of all, I thank you for my good luck charm. If it wasn't metal I would have crushed it in my clenched fist on the way here."

That brought a chuckle from him. "The horseshoe is not only for luck, but also to bring Ches to your mind. I have been counting the days until

251

you arrived. That's saying a lot, Val, because I have been so busy at work one day seems to fall into the next. It's been work, sleep, eat, in that order so that I could get it all done ahead of schedule to spend more time with you."

We pulled in front of Miss Eva's row house around two o'clock in the afternoon. I looked over at Ash. "Do I look like I've been crying?"

He stared at me. "No. They are the same pretty brown eyes I first saw at Stone's Chapel. That was one day I was happy I had gone to church."

The trees lining the street were in their lovely fall colors including a couple shrubs in her small fenced in yard. This was going to be my place of residence for a while. I prayed it would all work out, but what if it didn't? The thought was pushed to the back of my mind. I couldn't worry about that now.

Chapter 47

My work space at Fox Fashions was in the design room with JC Fox and a man named Kenneth Keys. I had my own desk and filing cabinet. JC and Kenneth had desks on the left side of the cramped room. Mine was to the right next to a large storage closet. The closet allowed me semi-privacy, and I used the side of it next to my desk to tack up notes and a calendar to keep on schedule. In contrast to this workroom, the show rooms in front were tastefully and expensively decorated, but this office was drab without any adornment. However, I didn't have time to gawk at anything that might prove a distraction.

It was my second week of work, and I was beginning to feel more comfortable with the city, work, and Miss Eva. Ash had shown me how to take the trolley to get to Fox Fashions. I didn't deviate from my route, therefore I was oblivious to the rest of Washington. My work day began at eight o'clock in the morning and I returned to Miss Eva's around six o'clock in the evening. I didn't have time to get homesick.

I quickly realized why Channing Fox was so eager to have me employed. The former designer had quit and had taken a position in New York City. It was close to November and the ladies of

Washington were getting ready for Christmas balls and Christmas teas. I was designated to design formal wear, which was my favorite. I had all the materials and trimmings I could imagine. It was up to the pattern makers and seamstresses to put it together.

JC's position was to design sportswear. The modern day women of the 20's were into tennis, golf, bicycling and swimming, but none of these were suited to the winter season so JC had time on his hands. He also helped his father in the shop. The ladies liked JC. He was always upbeat with the kind of flattery that made him sound sincere. It didn't hurt that he was a good-looking young man. The ladies left with a wide smile and a slimmer pocketbook.

Kenneth was in his late thirties, a bachelor with effeminate ways. He was of average height with a shock of light-brown hair, rather large nose, and narrowly set brown eyes, which looked like saucers under his thick glasses. Kenneth had an annoying habit of clearing his throat. I'm not exactly sure what Kenneth did because he was secretive about his work. I assumed he designed everyday wear. Kenneth also helped JC, who was usually late for work or busy in the shop. Except for the annoying habit of throat clearing, he worked efficiently and quietly and did not interrupt my concentration like JC did. JC was always kidding around. I'm not sure that set well with Kenneth, whose conversation with me was limited to "Good morning Miss Brown" and "Good evening Miss Brown."

As for Miss Eva, she was so prim and proper I felt like I was walking on egg shells in her presence. She had a maid twice a week and a lady come in to prepare dinner every evening except Sunday.

The past two Sundays were the only time I had seen Ash. He came to Miss Eva's and drove us to her Episcopal church, which was not much larger than Stone's Chapel. After the service, he took us out for brunch in a lovely hotel, which impressed Miss Eva. Perhaps I should have been also, but I felt the place a bit too stiff.

Ash and I had spent two hours together last Sunday afternoon. He was as swamped with his work as I was with mine. Ash was proud that his Senators won the World Series and he gave me a souvenir to give to Luke.

I spent most evenings in my upstairs room sketching for the ladies of Washington. They came in all sizes and shapes. It was important to design clothes that accented their best features or tamed down the less attractive parts, which meant I was learning which materials were suited to the design. This was far different than sitting on the back porch sketching for the fun of it.

Today when I arrived at Miss Eva's, the little lady held a big smile and an envelope in her hand. "The postman dropped a letter for you from your sister."

Those words were enough to lift my spirits. "I'll open it after dinner," I said.

"Vallie dear. You may open it right now. I'm sure you're eager to get news of home. Lila has left us a sumptuous pork roast and baked yams. You read your letter and I'll put the settings on the table." Dinner at Miss Eva's meant china, silver, crystal, freshly brewed tea and linen napkins. She was not being pretentious, that was Miss Eva's way. I was getting used to it and could handle the fine china without feeling I was going to break it. After all, I had worked at Lockwood and helped Miss Peg with many formal affairs. Miss Eva May set the table, but I was the one who cleaned up. That was the least I could do as she would only accept seven dollars a week for room and board.

While she fussed around putting the table just right, I opened Nora's letter.

October 23, 1924
Dear Vallie,

It seems as though you've been gone for months. All of us here at home trust you are doing well as we haven't heard otherwise.

The boys put apples away for winter and Mother and I put up jars of applesauce and apple butter. I've made many apple desserts. I took some apple tarts to Reverend Stephens and he inquired as to how you are doing. He is so different than when he is the minister. He said there will be a Presbyterian conference in Washington some time in November. I gave him Miss Eva's address thinking you would like to see someone from home. That is, if he goes to the conference, and if he gets some free time.

Lucy and Davey miss your stories and nursey rhymes. I do my best to fill in, but it's not the same.

As for Mark and Luke, they are kept busy with school and farm work. Mark is taking wonderful care of Ches, so you may rest assured that your beloved horse is contented. I'm sure you miss him.

I have made curtains for Billy's place and I would like to do a lot more as I know time will pass quickly and our wedding is only four months away. Billy says as soon as those six months Mother insisted on are over, we're getting hitched. I had to laugh. Unfortunately, my days are full and I have little time for the pleasures in life.

I almost forgot, Mother and I are making rum fruitcakes for Christmas. I'm not sure where the rum came from, but Mother keeps a lot of interesting stuff in her locked medical cabinet in the pantry.

This isn't much of a letter, but I want you to know that we are

thinking of you and pray you are
happy with your work.

        With my love,

        Nora

For the first time since I'd arrived in Washington I felt a hollow feeling in my stomach. I could picture Mother and Nora hurrying around the kitchen to get dinner on the table, while Father and the boys would be washing up and eager to eat. I missed the hub-bub of home.

"Vallie dear," Miss Eva called. "The table is ready. You may get the meal out of the oven."

I put Nora's letter in my pocket and went to have dinner with Miss Eva.

"How is everything at home?" she asked.

"Nora says all is well," I replied. I wouldn't let on that word from home gave me the feeling of nostalgia. I pulled the pork roast from the oven, piled the baked yams on a flowered plate, put green beans in an oval dish and placed all on a tray. "Miss Eva, Lila has made a delicious meal for us. There is tapioca pudding for dessert."

Even though there were only two of us, Miss Eva insisted on being the hostess. She sliced the meat and placed a piece of it, yams and green beans on our plates before we settled down for a quiet dinner. What a contrast from home. Would I ever get used to this?

Chapter 48

JC came to my desk. "You've got a challenge coming."

I looked up at him. "Why is that? Are you trying to unnerve me?"

He chuckled. "You don't strike me as the type to become unnerved, Val." He perched on the edge of my desk. "One of the congressional wives is coming to look for a ball gown. She's a big lady, and I mean big." He held his arms in a wide circle. "She has a tendency to find fault with everything."

I smiled. "She doesn't sound like a happy woman. Use your charming ways to soften her up."

JC laughed. "Speaking of my charming ways, there's a party Saturday night. Do you want to go?"

"No, thank you."

"Ash will be there," he said and examined my face to see my reaction.

I did my best not to let my disappointment show. "Then you should both have a good time," I said. "If you don't mind JC, I have a lot of work to do."

"That's your problem, Val. You spend too much time on work. You need to have fun, get out to see the rest of the world. When's your sister Nora coming to town?"

I gave him a cocky answer. "After she gets married."

"What a waste," said JC as he danced out the door. A quick glance across the room at Kenneth Keys told me he had taken in the whole exchange, which he didn't find entertaining. I found Kenneth to be a strange man.

JC said I needed to have fun. What was fun to me? As I thought about it, fun to me was: riding Ches, sketching on the back porch, visiting with Miss Fannie, reading stories and nursery rhymes to Lucy and Davey, evening chats with Nora in our upstairs bedroom, the little things in life that bring pleasure. It did cause me to wonder if I really liked what I was doing. Or, was it that I liked earning my own money, getting out of farm work and cleaning houses. When I had some free time I was going to sort it all out.

On Sunday, Ash picked us up for church service and we had brunch at the same place. Miss Eva looked forward to Sunday mornings. At least she had something to look forward to. She was fond of Ashton, as she called him. I suspected she also liked that he was a step up in the Washington scene.

Ash and I went walking in the afternoon. It was November and the trees had lost most of their leaves. The sun was out, there was no breeze. We piled up a big heap of leaves with our arms and took turns jumping in them. Then we threw them up in the air and let them shower over us. It was just plain fun and it was so good to laugh. I don't think I had felt that carefree since arriving in Washington. People who were strolling the paths and saw us playing in the leaves either laughed, shook their heads, or looked the other way. We didn't care.

There was a park bench near so we sat on it to rest up. He picked a couple of leaf fragments from the back of my hair.

"Did you have a good time last night?" I asked.

Ash looked at me with a frown. "What do you mean?"

"JC said you were going to a party."

He shrugged. "JC has a big mouth. He said he asked you to go and you refused."

"I did. The party scene doesn't appeal to me," I said.

He nodded. "That's why I didn't ask you. It's beginning not to appeal to me either."

We sat in silence watching the Potomac flow by. I loved the river and the peaceful setting. Best of all was having Ash beside me. It didn't bother me that he went to the party or if he was a hit with the young ladies. Ash and I enjoyed our time together.

"What do you think of JC?" he asked.

I couldn't help but smile. "I like him. He's always in a good mood."

He took my hand in his. "I'm glad you didn't go to the party with him."

I didn't answer. We sat in silence for a few minutes watching the river until Ash said, "Let's go to O'Brien's and get something to eat."

I looked over at him. "You don't have to ask me twice."

Ash stood and gave me a hand up.

"I'll race you to the car," I said, and took off running.

He let me get a distance and then ran past me. He was standing at the car with the door open when I got there. With a flourishing bow, he said. "My lady, your carriage awaits."

I caught my breath and gave a fancy curtsey. "Thank you, kind sir."

I stepped up on the running board and swung into the passenger's seat. "I'm starved."

"So am I," he replied. "It's probably from acting like a couple of five-year-olds."

"But wasn't it fun?"

"It was exhilarating," he said as he leaned over and kissed my cheek.

I was in heaven.

Chapter 49

It was the Friday before Thanksgiving when I arrived at the townhouse from a tiring day to find Reverend Stephens and Miss Eva chatting in the parlor. I had forgotten that Nora wrote that he might come by.

"Vallie, dear. Come right in. We have a visitor."

Wendell Stephens arose. "I had some free time after my conference," he said in an apologetic voice.

"We're pleased you came." I said, although when I read Nora's letter, I wasn't thrilled with the aspect of him visiting. It was good to see someone from home.

"Lila has left us a wonderful chicken dinner with all the trimmings," Miss Eva said. "Vallie dear, you may set it out as I have the table ready."

"May I be of help?" Wendell asked.

"You are our guest, but you may act as the host," Miss Eva replied.

I doubted that the reverend was up to the task of cutting up chicken and fixing our plates. I thought it an imposition on Miss Eva's part.

"I'd be happy to," he answered. The three of us went to the dining room where the table was glowing with Eva's fine preparation.

He seated Miss Eva, turned to me and said, "Vallie, I'll help bring in the dishes."

Feeling a jolt of anxiety, I led him into the kitchen. I hadn't said a word, but my apprehension must have shown because he whispered, "I'll bet you don't think I can do this."

I could feel my face burn. We placed the dishes on two trays and carried them into the dining room. He seated me and took his place at the head of the table, said some words of grace and began slicing the chicken and passing our plates. I was amazed. This was the man who always seemed to question himself.

After a delicious dinner of baked chicken, mashed potatoes, dressing, gravy and fresh dinner rolls, we adjourned to the parlor. We talked a bit about his Presbyterian conference before Miss Eva excused herself. "Reverend Stephens, I am delighted that you took the time to stop by. Now, if you young people will excuse me, I am rather tired after that big meal."

Wendell rose from his chair and offered her an arm up. "I'm sure you are, Miss Eva. I thank you for your hospitality."

"You are welcome any time," she said and went to her room.

He turned to me. "Vallie, I'll help you clean up and then let's go out. I know a great little jazz place."

Lucky I didn't swoon because I was taken completely off guard. "I don't know anything about jazz," was the only reply I could make.

"I think you'll like it. C'mon. Let's get this place cleaned up. I have to go back to being the straight-laced Presbyterian minister tomorrow, and I want to leave Washington on an enjoyable note."

He was calling me by my first name, but I didn't know what to call him. Preacher didn't seem to fit. "Am I permitted to call you Wendell?" I asked.

"Call me Ted, that's what my friends and family call me. My name is Theodore Wendell, not Windy Wendell," he said with a wink.

My second embarrassment for the evening. "Where did you hear that?"

"Word gets around," he replied.

"I might as well be honest," I said. "You know I hinted that you should shorten your sermons, but I didn't want to come right out and say it."

"I'm trying," he replied.

Perhaps I should get to know this Ted Stephens because I was quite sure I knew the Reverend Stephens. Or did I? Ted Stephens piqued my curiosity. The tiredness I felt when I arrived was gone, and the thought of going to my room to draw more sketches didn't appeal to me. Maybe it was time I learned about jazz, I reasoned with myself.

Reverend Stephens had rented a horse and buggy. It was not snazzy like Ash's sports coupe, but I hadn't ridden in a buggy for quite some time. Ted Stephens gave me a hand as I stepped up to take my seat.

"There's a carriage robe in the back if you need it," he offered.

"No thanks. I'm fine right now," I replied. "This is fun," I said. "It feels so good to ride in the open air."

"Tell me about your job, Vallie. Do you like it and are you happy you've made the change? It's a big step for you."

I had to think about it for a moment. "Yes, I do. It has its good points and bad points like most jobs, but Mr. Fox is pleased with my work and the ladies of Washington haven't voiced complaints. Sometimes I have to change my design to satisfy their ideas. That is irksome because I know my design is better. And, one of the male designers in the room is a strange duck."

Ted Stephens laughed. "We males come in all forms," he said.

"Do you remember meeting Ashton Corbin this summer?" I asked.

He nodded as he turned the horse down another lighted street. "A nephew of Vern and Elsie Corbin, if I remember correctly."

"He has been a god-send to me or I might have just turned around and taken the next train back to Bluemont."

He chuckled. "It's good you have a mentor here in this capital city."

I could hear the music before we went into the place. Inside we were ushered to a table for two. The room was dim, warm, not large, and very plain. It appeared people, black and white sitting together in one room, came here to relax and listen to the music.

Calling the minister Ted seemed foreign to me, so I tried not to use his name if I didn't have to. As the evening progressed, he was mesmerized by the sound of jazz and all conversation stopped. I enjoyed the music, although I'm not sure I understood it.

We were there for over an hour. When the group took a break, Ted said it was time to leave as he had the early train to catch. I was all for it because I was getting tired. The boy brought the horse and buggy around to the front and we climbed in.

This time he pulled the robe from the back and placed it over my lap. "It's going to be a chilly ride," he said. "So what do you think of jazz?" he asked as he got into the driver's seat.

I looked over at him and shrugged. "I don't know. It's different."

He chucked to the horse and grinned. "It grows on a person. I used to play the saxophone."

I felt my eyebrows raise. What was this man going to surprise me with next?

Rather than to pry into his former life as a saxophone player, I asked, "How are things at home?"

"Nothing changes too much. It was a good crop season for the farmers. Billy and Nora are making wedding plans, and Fannie and Jess Edwards want to have Daniel baptized at Christmas. I much prefer baptisms to funerals," he said.

"Have you seen my horse, Ches? I do miss him."

He looked over at me with a faint smile. "I'm sure you do. He's like your best friend. I see Mark riding him sometimes."

The thought of my beloved horse brought a lump to my throat. I wanted to talk to him, feel his smooth body and throw a saddle over him for a ride across the fields and let him drink from the Longmarsh Run.

We were almost to Miss Eva's row house. "I've brought a small package in the back your mother sent for Thanksgiving. She has invited me to share the big meal."

"I hate the thought of not being home. Are you accepting Mother's invitation?"

"I wouldn't miss it," he replied. "Between your mother's delicious cooking and Nora's desserts, I'll probably gain five pounds."

I had to chuckle. Ted Stephens could tack on five pounds and it would never show. "I hate not being home for Thanksgiving, but I will be home for Christmas. Right now I am so busy with work that I cannot come home."

"How will you spend the day?" he asked.

I shrugged. "I really don't know."

We stopped in front of Miss Eva's and he removed the lap robe and tossed it in the back. "I'm very pleased that you came with me this evening," he said. "I can report to your parents that you look well."

I had to smile. I'll bet he doesn't report that we spent the evening listening to a jazz band, I thought.

Ted came around the side of the buggy and gave me a hand down before he pulled the small box from the back seat and walked me to the door. Miss Eva had left it unlocked so I opened it.

He handed me the package. "Don't get consumed with your work, Vallie. Washington has much to offer. This has been a good respite for me, and I can go back taking on the role of minister. I will look forward to seeing you at Christmas."

I stood in the doorway and watched him go. When he wasn't the Reverend Stephens, he was a different person. It made me wonder why he chose the ministry. I knew nothing of his background, but I found Ted Stephens interesting, and one day I was determined to find out.

Chapter 50

Thanksgiving Day of 1924 was the loneliest day I had ever spent, even though Mother had sent pickled beets, wild grape jam, and molasses cookies in the package Reverend Stephens had brought. It was Miss Eva Lou and I having dinner together. Lila had left us sliced turkey and all the trimmings that constituted a Thanksgiving dinner, but it felt nothing like Thanksgiving. At home, Nora and Mother would have been cooking for three days. There would be the smell of baking turkey and fresh bread filling the warm kitchen. There would be noisy children and obnoxious teenaged brothers trying to sneak a snippet of food and Mother shooing them out of the kitchen.

The gravity of how much I missed home hit me like a blow to the stomach. Washington was quiet, Ash was spending the day with his family, the Fox family was going to a fancy restaurant, and I was stuck with Miss Eva Lou. I did owe her for showing my sketches to Mr. Fox, and for allowing me to rent a room. Perhaps spending Thanksgiving with her was some kind of repayment.

"Vallie dear, would you like the honor of being the Hostess?" she asked.

I found no honor in throwing food on a plate, but I smiled at her and said I would be happy to assume that position. This pleased her so I figured I had done my duty for the day. She said grace and we sat down to a quiet and delicious dinner. Afterwards, I cleaned up, then excused myself before I went to my room to work on designs.

While I was drawing up some lovely sketches for New Year's Eve festivities, it occurred to me that I would be home for Christmas and maybe extend my stay through the first of the year. The thought brightened my somber mood and gave me impetus to create for the ladies of Washington. I decided I was going to talk with Mr. Fox for permission to take ten days away from Fox Fashions.

I slept well knowing I had a plan in place. One that would cure my increasing desire to be home.

The next day I seemed to walk with a lighter step. The shop was already humming with activity when I arrived. Kenneth Keys was at his desk, clearing his throat as he had a habit of doing. It didn't seem to annoy me as much today. JC was late and his mother had stopped by to check up on him.

"Have you seen JC?" she asked me.

"Not this morning, ma'am," I replied.

"When he comes in, tell him that he is to report to me as soon as he arrives." With that said, she turned on her heel and walked out of the room.

Kenneth looked over at me and said, "Looks like JC's in hot water again."

Kenneth actually saying a sentence to me took me by surprise, but I nodded and kept my attention to my work.

When JC came in the door I told him that he was to report to the main office right away. "You look awful," I said. "Did you have a fight with the turkey?"

"Very funny, I had a big Thanksgiving party. My head hurts." He did look uncomfortable.

"That's why I don't like your parties. Was Ash there," I asked, trying to sound nonchalant.

"No. Somebody said he has a cold. He's not much of a party-goer anymore. He's still got that crazy idea he's good enough to pitch for the Senators."

I shrugged. "Maybe he is. At least he has a goal to work toward."

"Meaning I don't?" JC said.

"Meaning nothing," I replied. "You'd better get to see your parents before they fire you."

"Sometimes I wish they would," he said and left the room.

I glanced over at Kenneth and could tell he had taken in every word.

Chapter 51

A week later, fingering the good luck charm Ash had given me, I was standing in the small office of Channing Fox. He looked up as I entered. "What can I do for you, Miss Brown?"

I assumed my bravest stance. "I would like to spend Christmas at home."

He shrugged his shoulders. "I don't see why not," he replied. "We don't work on Christmas."

"Well sir, the fact is, I would like to be gone for ten days."

He didn't answer right away leaving an uncomfortable silence. Then he said, "I run a business here. Time is money and I can't afford to have my employees running off for ten days at a time."

I was miffed. "I wouldn't be running off. The mad rush of Christmas will be over."

He shook his head. "Of course, but you're forgetting about New Year's Eve."

I had my answer ready. "I'm working on designs now. Besides, New Year's Eve is a younger crowd and JC is good at those fashions."

He nodded. "If he puts his mind to it."

"Kenneth can help him," I said. "I can work on designs at home. People don't shop much the week after Christmas." I wasn't sure of that, but I thought it bolstered my cause.

He leaned back in his chair and looked straight at me. "You are planning on coming back."

"Oh yes, sir," I answered, "I promise that if I ever want to leave I will give you a two week notice. I won't leave you flat like your last designer."

He chuckled. "So you heard about that."

I felt my face blush.

He sat for a long silent moment. "Well, Miss Brown. I suppose we can manage without you over the holidays. You may leave on the 24th, but I want you right back here the day after the new year begins."

My joy was obvious as I offered a wide smile. "Thank you, sir. I'll be back and ready to start the new year."

I left his office and almost flew to the design room. JC looked at me when I entered. "What put that rosy glow in your cheeks?" he asked.

I didn't hesitate to answer, "Your father has given me from Christmas to New Year's off. I'm going home for the holidays."

"You're going to miss some big parties," he said.

I shook my head. "I won't miss a thing," I replied. "Being home for ten days will be one big party."

"Maybe I should come out and see what makes you so giddy about that place. Is Nora going to be there?"

I shot him a disgusted look. "I told you she's engaged to be married."

He shook his head. "What a shame."

That evening as Miss Eva Lou and I were finishing our meal, there was a knock on the front door.

"I'll get it," I said.

What a pleasant surprise to see Ash standing there dressed in a three-piece black suit, white shirt and dark tie. He wore a plaid driver's cap. I hadn't seen him since before Thanksgiving.

"Ash!" I exclaimed. "How good to see you."

"I hope I'm not coming at an inconvenient time," he apologized.

"Not at all. We just finished dinner. Come in. Miss Eva will be happy to see you." I opened the door wider for him to enter.

Ash removed his cap and handed me a box. "I brought dessert," he said.

I led him to the dining room where Miss Eva was still sitting in her chair.

"Look who was at the door," I said to her.

A wide grin appeared on her aging face. "Ashton! We have missed you. I hope you have been well."

"I was under the weather with a nasty cold, but I'm back at work."

"Ash has brought us dessert, Miss Eva. Shall I put water over for tea?"

"Certainly, Vallie dear. Now, Ashton you come and sit right next to me and tell me how things are with your parents and what you have been up to in your absence."

I went to the kitchen to prepare the tea and dessert while Miss Eva Lou had Ash all to herself. How fortunate for her, I thought. I could hear the din of conversation as I prepared the tea. Then I placed the dessert on Miss Eva's treasured china plates. I felt nervous and handling her fine china made me more so. I would never forgive myself if I accidently broke a piece.

When I returned to the dining room they were sharing a laugh.

Miss Eva looked up and spied the dessert. "Cream puffs! Ashton Corbin you are a wonder." He laughed.

"I hope the Senators feel the same way." I'm meeting with the manager to see if I can join them for spring training."

I served the tea and dessert. Ash stood and pulled out my chair and seated me at the table. It occurred to me that this was a good time to tell them both that I would be spending the holidays at our farm.

Ash looked disappointed. "Ten days?" he said.

"Yes. I'll leave on the 24th and return January 2nd. It will be so good to be home."

Miss Eva looked at Ash. "Ever since Reverend Stephens visited us, Vallie has had a yearning for home."

"Reverend Stephens visited?" he questioned.

"The minister at Stone's Chapel, you must remember him. He had a Presbyterian conference here in Washington," I told him.

He chuckled. "The one you called Windy Wendell?"

"That was unkind of me." I said. "He's really very nice. And, believe it or not, he likes to listen to jazz. I'm not sure he is comfortable in his role of tending to the flock."

Miss Eva shook her head. "That is such a difficult task."

Ash looked over at me and said, "It seems you have gotten to know him well."

I didn't look at him. "Better than I did," I said, and I finished my cream puff.

Chapter 52

On Sunday, Ash came in his yellow coupe to take me and Miss Eva to her church. We hadn't been to services since before Thanksgiving. Although I wasn't thrilled about sitting   through the hour long service, I was delighted to be sitting close to Ash in the car where we were shoulder to shoulder.

At church he seated Miss Eva first. She was always impressed with his good manners.

We had brunch at her favorite swanky place, and Ash drove us back to her row house. He took the key she offered, opened the door and ushered us inside.

"Ashton, thank you for a wonderful morning. Now, you two dears will have to excuse me as I feel I need to take a nap. I do believe I overfed myself at brunch," Miss Eva said.

Ash chuckled. "That's a bad habit of mine," he said. "It was good to have your company. If Vallie is up to it, we'll go and walk it off.

His words were music to my ears as I had not seen him for days. I buttoned my coat and took a scarf from the hall tree, pulled on my gloves, and said goodbye to Miss Eva.

Ash took my elbow and walked me to his car. When he got into the driver's seat he looked at me before he started it. "I've missed you, Val."

I looked over at him. "I've missed you too. When JC told me you had a cold, I prayed it wasn't something more serious."

"Kept me out of work for a few days." He started the car. "I'm sure you've been busy."

"Busier than I'd like to be, but the time passes quickly, and I'm looking forward to going home."

"How did you wrangle ten days off?" he asked.

I had to smile. "I convinced Mr. Fox that JC and Kenneth Keys can handle the New Year's crowd."

"He must like your work and wants to keep you happy," Ash said.

My smile deepened. "The ladies don't complain. They're a stuffy bunch."

He laughed. "You would probably put my parents in that category. I just think it's the Washington way."

"Where are we going?" I asked.

"Let's walk and look at the window decorations. I think they try to outdo each other with their Christmas ideas. Are you up to a brisk walk?"

"I'd like nothing better," I replied.

Ash pulled the car to the side of the road and we walked hand in hand up and down the streets of Washington. We laughed, giggled at toy soldiers, trains, dolls, and BB guns. At Woodward and Lothrop we were in awe of the window displays, which were like a walk through fantasy land. Never had I seen such wonder. Could I give all this up to return to the country life I knew?

I looked at Ash and said, "I believe my pocketbook is more suited to F.W. Woolworth."

"If you're going to take gifts to your family, we could go shopping one day," he offered.

"Ash, I'd love to. I'll have to find some items that I can pack easily." My thought was on the train ride home. I didn't want cumbersome packages.

"Val," he said, "I have work to catch up on, but I'm sure I can have it finished by Saturday. We can go Christmas shopping if you're free."

"I'll make sure I am." I said. That would give me two weeks before I returned home, so that I could have the gifts wrapped and packed and not have to worry about them. I didn't want any distractions or loose ends before I left.

After we finished our walk, we went to O'Brien's for hot chocolate and a doughnut. Even though O'Brien's was a popular spot, it seemed that Ash and I were the only ones in the place. We could tune out the din of the crowd and be in our own world. I relished those times.

Miss Eva's door was unlocked when we arrived at her town home. She was sitting in the parlor. "Did you have a good walk?" she asked.

"That we did," Ash answered. "Did you have a good nap?"

"Oh my, yes. Will you be coming for church next Sunday?" Miss Eva asked.

"I'd like to. Vallie and I are going Christmas shopping on Saturday. I will give you an answer then."

Miss Eva smiled at him. "I do enjoy our Sundays," she said.

Ash turned to leave. I went to the door where he hesitated for a moment before he took my hand and said, "I'll see you at ten on Saturday."

I felt he wanted to kiss me, but this was not the time or place.

Chapter 53

As I think about it, it's good that both Ash and I are busy with our work. The time passes quickly. I can look forward to the days I will spend at home, and he can look forward to baseball spring training, if he is lucky enough to make the cut.

I have to admit that I might care too much if we spent more time together. I wondered if he feels the same way. He certainly hasn't given me "the bum's rush", and I know he cares for me. I don't know how strong that is. And, of course, there's Mother's warning voice in the back of my mind, "Don't get too close."

Here it is Saturday an hour before he is to pick me up for Christmas shopping. I've had breakfast and I'm spending the time primping up to look my best and re-checking my list of names for presents to buy. For once in my life, I have extra money in my pocketbook. I think Mother would be proud of me or will she think my gift-giving extravagant? I won't worry about that now.

I was in the parlor and answered the door as soon as I heard the ring of the bell. Ash stood there looking dapper in his tan pants, and cable-knit sweater worn over a long-sleeved shirt. A red tie peeked through the V-neck of the cream-colored sweater. He carried a brown plaid driver's cap in his hand.

His wide smile when I opened the door told me he was glad to see me. I did like his smile. "Ready to go, Val?"

"I just need to get my coat. Will I need an umbrella?" I asked.

"I have one in the car, he said. "I believe it's one of those gray days that never develops into anything."

Miss Eva appeared while we were talking. "Ashton, how nice to see you. Vallie tells me you are taking her Christmas shopping."

"Oh, you must hit the prime department stores. When my husband was alive, we did so enjoy hunting for gifts, but those days are over for me now. You young people go and have a good time." She wasn't looking for sympathy, she was lamenting the loss of days gone by.

"Is there anything we can get for you while we're out?" Ash said.

She shook her head. "No, Ashton. You are a dear to be so considerate."

Ash helped me with my coat and we bid Miss Eva goodbye. In the car he looked over at me and said, "We are going to spend the whole day together. Just you and me. I've been waiting for today all week."

I had to smile. "So have I."

"Where do you want to go first?" he asked.

I shrugged. "You know the city, and I know I told you F.W. Woolworth was more suited to my means."

He nodded. "I remember, but it doesn't cost to browse. Sometimes there are good buys in the bargain basements of the more expensive stores."

"Lead the way," I told him. "My Christmas shopping has always been limited to Coyner's department store in Berryville, or Mr. White's general store, or Nora and I making candy and cookies for gifts."

He had started the car and we were on our way. "I thought you didn't like to cook."

"I don't, but making Christmas candy is fun, and it's only once a year. I can cook if I have to, but I'd rather leave it up to Nora and Mother. They are much better at it than I am."

He turned the corner at the end of the street. "I'll bet they can't sketch and design like you can. Don't sell yourself short, Val."

His words warmed my heart.

"Do you know what you want to look for?" Ash asked.

I chuckled. "I have a list of people but not a list of gifts. Anything that will fit in my suitcase."

"How about a pitcher's mitt for Luke? I know a good sports store. He needs a good glove and I need a new one."

I nodded.

The sports store was a novelty. Women were becoming more outward. So there were bicycles, tennis equipment, swim wear, and various clothing for the different sports. I found some swim suits daring, but Ash said they were for the serious swimmers in competitions. I couldn't imagine wearing a bathing suit that went above the knee.

We left the store with two mitts, a fancy slingshot for Mark, and a jump rope for Lucy.

As we walked to put the packages in the car, I said, "I wonder if JC knows about this place. He might get some ideas for designing."

Ash shrugged. "He's not much into sports, unless there's a shapely lady on the tennis court. I don't think his sketches are because he has your creative talent."

Ash opened the rumble seat and put our packages on the floor.

"I get the feeling you don't like JC," I said.

"He's all right. Not much ambition for where he's heading." He closed the rumble seat and looked at me. "Maybe I'm jealous because he gets to work with you all day."

I smiled. "He's good to me and lifts the spirit of the place. If it were just me and Kenneth Keys, I might not have lasted this long."

Ash laughed and took my hand. "I've met Kenneth. He's and odd duck, but not a threat for your affections."

I had to laugh. "He might surprise you."

Ash was amused. "I doubt it."

In Macy's bargain basement I found a puzzle for Davey, socks for Father, perfume for Nora, and a lovely scarf for Mother. For Miss Eva, I found a wool fringed shawl. I wasn't sure what to give Ash, and I couldn't buy something in his presence.

We were through by three o'clock. The presents were all tucked away in the car and we spent the rest of the time admiring the decorations.

There was no snow, but the air was crisp and invigorating. By five o'clock, we ended up in our favorite spot in O'Brien's.

When we left the evening air was chilly and dusk had set in. He opened the door of his car and I settled in before he got into the driver's seat.

I looked over at him and smiled. "It's cold," I said.

He put his arm around me, pulled me close and I was caught in the ecstasy of a tender kiss.

"That'll warm both of us up," he said. "I'm sorry if I'm out of line, but I've been wanting to kiss you for a long time, and it never seemed the time was right." His arm was still around me and I rested my head on his shoulder.

"Do you wonder what the future holds?" he asked.

"Sometimes," I answered. "I try not to think about it too much."

"If I make the Senators, I'll be traveling a lot."

I lifted my head from his shoulder and looked at him. "I know, but it's your dream, Ash. You can't let anything get in the way of not fulfilling it."

He looked straight ahead. "I know, but I like you a lot, Val. I don't want us to drift apart."

"You can write letters and so can I." Wasn't I being the brave one?

His tone was serious, "Do you think going home is going to change your mind about living and working in Washington?"

I was honest. "It might. But I'm not cut out to be a farm wife. When Nora gets married, I worry about Mother taking on all the burden."

He thought for a moment. "You could hire someone to help her."

I shook my head, "She would never agree to that."

"Probably not," he said.

Then he looked over at me and smiled. "Let's not talk about this anymore. I don't want to dampen our wonderful day." He started the car and headed in the direction of Miss Eva's row house.

"Ash, I do thank you. This has been a day to remember. You are such a help to me."

"One day I hope I'm more than that."

Secretly, I hoped he would be too. I didn't know what the future would bring, but I did know that I wanted more of Ashton Corbin's kisses.

Chapter 54

Union Station was a throng of travelers. Ash found a place to park about a block from there. Before we got out of the car, he reached behind the seat and pulled out a gaily wrapped present and handed it to me. "Merry Christmas, Val."

I was delighted. I reached into my pocketbook and took out a wrapped gift for him.

Ash was surprised, but I could see he was pleased. "Let's open them."

I unwrapped mine first. "How beautiful!" Inside my package, I found a pair of soft kidskin gloves trimmed with mink fur cuffs. I rubbed the smooth silky fur against my cheek. "Oh, Ash. These are so pretty." I leaned over and kissed his cheek.

"I'm glad you like them. They will keep your hands warm. Now it's my turn."

When he unwrapped and opened the box he gave a low whistle. Inside was a silver pocket knife inlaid with turquoise. "Val, I'll keep it forever."

"I had JC pick it out for me. Father always says that a man needs a handy knife in his pocket."

He looked over at me with a pensive smile and then he kissed me. "I'm going to miss you."

We left the car and he carried my suitcase. I carried my pocketbook and tote bag. But we made sure we had one free arm so we could walk hand in hand before I boarded the train.

Inside the train car I sat next to a window where I could see Ash. He waved at me and I waved back as the train chugged out of Union Station headed for Bluemont. With mixed feelings, it was good I was on my way. I was eager to get home and disappointed to have to leave Ash.

All the way through the hamlets and up the mountain my mind was absorbed with muddled thoughts of Ash, work, Washington and Miss Eva. I knew I couldn't impinge on her generosity too much longer. I fingered the good luck charm Ash had given me, which helped relieve my anxiety.

Billy and Nora were waiting for me when I alighted the train. My knees felt a little wobbly after the long ride. Nora rushed ahead of Billy and gave me a bear hug. "I am so glad you're here! We've all missed you."

Billy smiled. "Hi, Vallie. The truck is waiting. I'll tuck your suitcase under a blanket in the back."

Nora and I walked arm in arm.

She talked about their wedding plans and although they thought a Christmas wedding would be nice, Mother convinced them otherwise.

"So, we'll get married in the spring. That will give you time to design a wedding dress for me," Nora said.

That gave me a start. "I haven't designed wedding dresses," I said.

She looked at me and smiled. "Then this will be your first."

When we turned down the lane to the farm house, I felt my heart race. I was back home again at last. What a great feeling.

Father and the boys were busy doing chores, but they came out when they heard the rumbling of Billy's prized truck. I hugged each of them and the smell of the barn permeated my senses. I didn't even care if the barn smell got into my clothes.

Then Davey and Lucy came running from the house and I corralled them in my arms. Mother waited on the back steps. I let the young ones go and hurried to see her. Mother hugged me tight without a word. I could tell she was holding back tears.

Lucy and Davey bolted up the steps. "Vallie, Mother wouldn't let us trim the tree until you got here," Lucy said.

"Yeah," Davey chimed in. "Hurry up Vallie."

Not much had changed with them.

With the help of Billy and Nora we trimmed the tree before Mother called Nora and me to set the table for dinner. It was suppertime and the barn workers would be hungry. Mother had made a big pot of stew and fresh bread.

I didn't realize how hungry I was until I started to eat. It had been a long day. After grace was said everyone wanted to hear about my time in the city. As I related my tale, I could see disappointment on my Mother's face when I told them how helpful Ash had been. Perhaps I smiled too much at the mention of his name. That's the way I felt and Mother would just have to accept it.

That evening when Nora and I were getting ready for bed, I told her JC asked about her. She chuckled.

"Vallie I've never had a fling, but I'll bet I could have one with JC."

"Nora! You don't sound like a woman who is about to be married," I said. "Don't let Mother hear you talk like that."

With a slight toss of her head and a shrug of her shoulder, she said, "No, I know my place. I'm not the daring sort. It sounds as though you see a lot of Ash. How do you feel about him?"

I sat on the edge of the bed in my nightgown. "I wouldn't be telling the truth if I said I didn't care for him. I do and he cares for me. That's my problem and one I hope to sort out while I'm here."

Nora had finished brushing her hair and came to sit across from me on her bed. "Mother thinks he's in a higher status in life and you're going to be crushed when he finds someone in his class."

"I know his family is of the social set. I've never met them, but I can tell by things he says, and by his circle of friends. Washington is all about social climbing. Ash isn't like that. He still wants to be a big league pitcher." I wasn't sure Nora was convinced.

"I guess that's a problem you have to work out for yourself," she said.

Chapter 55

Christmas morning I was up before anyone. It was light enough outside because of a full moon. I left the room quietly so that I didn't wake Nora.

I was careful to go down the stairs stepping where I knew they didn't creak. I never knew the house to be so quiet and still, where at Miss Eva's it was always like that. I don't think I'd ever get used to the silence.

Dressed in my flannel nightgown and wool knee socks, I pulled on my boots, picked up a lump of sugar, threw on my warm farm jacket and went to see Ches. He was in his stall and scrambled to his feet when I opened the barn door. To my eyes he was a beautiful sight.

I opened the stall, went in and threw my arms around his neck. "Oh, my wonderful friend, I have missed you so much." He turned his head and nuzzled my shoulder. "We're going to go on a long ride after church." I sat on a pile of hay and gave him the sugar treat. "I wish you could talk," I said to my horse. "You could help me with my jumbled thoughts." The smell of the stall, warmth of Ches, and a comfortable spot on the hay seemed to mesmerize my senses. I leaned back on the wood side and fell asleep.

I startled awake to someone gently shaking my shoulder. "Vallie, you'd best wake up. We'll be going to services pretty soon."

In my sleepy haze I opened my eyes and saw Father smiling down at me. "You must be tired from your train ride."

I tried to rub the sleep from them and then stretched my arms. Father offered me a calloused hand and pulled me to my feet. "I didn't mean to fall asleep. I just had to come out and see Ches."

"Mark has taken good care of him, but your horse will be happy to have you back. Now, you run along. We don't want to be late."

I hurried to the house and went into the kitchen. The warmth from the wood stove and mingled odors of coffee and breakfast foods were pleasing. These little everyday things I had been missing for the few months I was in the city.

"I'm sorry, Mother. I went out to see Ches and fell asleep."

"Well, hurry on up and get dressed for church. Nora has the young ones ready. Father and the boys will be here in a few minutes. We don't want to be late for services."

Personally, I didn't care if we missed church.

"Reverend Stephens said he had a nice visit with you and Miss Eva Lou when he was in Washington," Mother said as I headed to the dry sink set in an alcove at the bottom of the staircase.

"Yes, it was good of him to stop." I smiled to myself. Reverend Stephens, the man whose friends

293

and family called him Ted, and the man who loved to listen to jazz. Was he going to be in the role of Windy Wendell of Stone's Chapel?

In my room, I tossed my nightgown and knee socks on the floor and dressed for church. I was brushing my hair when Nora came into the room. "Mother says it's time to eat."

"I'm ready. Does my hair smell like the barn?"

Nora sniffed it and shook her head. "It smells like toilet water."

"That's because I dabbed toilet water in it," I replied.

We scurried down the stairs. Mother had put a large platter of bacon, ham, eggs and grits on the table. "Nora, bring the bowl of potatoes," Mother ordered.

We sat down. Father said grace and we filled our plates. The only sound in the kitchen was the noise of the Brown family hungrily eating a sumptuous breakfast. Mother's food was far tastier than the Sunday morning brunches in that expensive restaurant in Washington.

I heard Billy Wood's farm truck coming down the lane. "Vallie, you can ride with us," Nora said.

The day was pleasant, not too cold, but crisp enough for gloves and a scarf. "When I pulled on my kidskin gloves, Nora took in a deep breath and put her hands in mine to feel the smoothness. "Vallie, they are beautiful."

We were in the kitchen ready to leave. "Ash gave them to me."

I saw a grimace come over Mother's face.

At Stone's Chapel we waited for Father to seat us in our usual pew. Billy and Nora sat in the one ahead of us. The chapel was always noisy with people getting settled into the uncomfortable wood bench seats. We sat like stone statues once the service began because every little movement would be magnified in the cavernous interior. No children were allowed in the small balcony in the rear of the chapel. That could lead to disaster. Once an older member fell asleep and we heard his loud snoring until someone woke him up.

The organist hit the keys and we stood for the opening hymn. It was Christmas and we would sing the heartwarming carols of the Lord's birthday.

When Reverend Stephens entered, I was sure he saw me, but he gave no recognition. It was after the service that he   called me back to the front steps once the rest of the members had cleared.

"Vallie, I'm glad to see you. Will you be here for a few days?"

I nodded. "I have to be back in Washington on the second of January."

"I'd like to talk with you," he said. "When would be a good time?"

I had to think as I hadn't given much time to planning out my stay. There were people I wanted to visit. "Today is going to be full of Christmas."

"I realize you have catching up to do," he said. "Perhaps tomorrow."

I thought about it for a couple of seconds. "I promised Ches a long ride today, but I don't think I can fit it in. Let's go tomorrow."

"Good," he said. "My horse can use some exercise. I'll ride over to your place after lunch. It's important that I talk with you," he said.

I left to join Billy and Nora in the truck. "What was that about?" asked Nora.

"Reverend Stephens and I are going horseback riding tomorrow. He wants to talk to me. I'm not sure why."

"That ought to cause a stir," said Nora.

"Reverend Stephens and Miss Brown going riding? That should put a little spice in the life of the gossipers," Billy said.

Nora and I laughed.

However, it did make me wonder what Ted Stephens wanted to talk about.

Chapter 56

Ted Stephens was dressed for riding when he arrived around one o'clock in the afternoon. He was tall and slim and looked noble in jodhpurs, cropped jacket, knee-high leather boots and warm cap.

Mother answered his knock. "Reverend Stephens! I am surprised."

"Hello, Mrs. Brown. Vallie and I are going horseback riding. Both of our horses need the exercise. Didn't she tell you?"

I came down the stairs and saw Mother was flustered. "I'm sorry, Mother. I should have told you that Reverend Stephens was coming by today."

She looked at me under hooded brows. "Yes, you should have."

Mother was dressed for house cleaning, and she always wanted to look her best when we had visitors.

Her angst was short-lived. "I'll have a nice meal ready for you when you return," she said.

I had pulled on Jake's old trousers under my riding skirt and wore my wool jacket with a wool hat. I pulled on my worn leather riding gloves and we left the house to go to the barn to saddle Ches.

Ted's horse was a handsome roan. He led her by the reins as we walked together. "I hope I didn't upset your mother," he said.

"It was inconsiderate of me not to remember to tell her you were coming, but yesterday was such a flurry of activity, it completely slipped my mind."

He smiled. "I have days like that."

He helped me bridle and saddle Ches and we were on our way. "Which way are we going?" I asked.

"Let's ride down by the Opequon. There's a pretty spot there where we can talk."

We went through the fields and up and down hills until we got to the creek. I rode behind Ted because he knew where he wanted to go. When we reached the spot, I could see why he had chosen it. The ground sloped down to the water. There were trees and vines overhanging giving privacy from the outside world.

"I've lived here all my life and I've never found this place," I said.

He shrugged. "Guess I'm an adventurer."

We got off our horses and it took me a minute to stabilize my legs. It had been months since I'd ridden and I knew I was going to be sore tomorrow.

We tethered our horses to some thick bushes and sat side by side on a tree log smoothed by once being in the water. "Did you make this bench?" I asked.

He laughed. "You can hardly call it a bench. I hauled it out after a heavy rain had sent it downstream. Ingenious, don't you think?"

"Resourceful," I said. "What's so important that you wanted to talk about?"

He threw a stone into the creek, then came to sit beside me on the smooth log. "I'm going to leave the ministry."

For some unknown reason, I wasn't surprised. "Why?"

"It was that evening I spent with you when we went to listen to the jazz band."

That did surprise me. "What did that have to do with it?"

He leaned forward and clasped his hands together between his thighs. "I had a brother a year older than me and we were inseparable. We loved music, played in a small band with friends, and he and I were going to open a music shop. He was more talented than me."

He stopped. I waited patiently because I knew it wasn't the time to talk.

After a couple of long minutes, he continued, "Tom got killed in a motorcycle accident. I told him those bikes weren't safe, but he was kind of a daredevil."

"Is that why you went into the ministry? Did you think God was punishing you in some way?"

"I was devastated. I don't know what I thought, but I was in a sad state until our minister helped pull me out of my depression." He sat up and looked over at me. "That was a dark time, Vallie. I guess I thought that if the minister had helped me, I could help others who had troubles."

"Why are you telling me this?"

"Because I think you will understand. I know you're torn between your career in Washington and wanting to be home. I also know that you are fond of Ashton Corbin, and you are unsure of your feelings."

That caused my head to snap in his direction and my eyes opened wide. "How do you know that?"

"Because I've seen you together at the chapel, and when we went to the jazz place, you said he was going to try out for the Senators training camp because he wants to be a big league pitcher."

"That doesn't mean anything," I countered.

"Yes, it does. If he makes the big leagues, he'll be traveling a lot, meeting new people. His family is well-respected in the Washington set, and you're concerned you might not meet their qualifications."

I was chagrined. "What makes you such an expert?"

"My family is from the same social strata. Running a music shop is far below their expectations. But, I've made up my mind that's what I'm going to do."

I shrugged. "Mother is the one who is concerned I'm going to get hurt if I 'get too close' as she likes to say."

"We have to make our own decisions. Trust yourself to follow where the path leads. You won't be happy unless you do." He stood and offered me a hand up, "That's what I wanted to talk about. Your last sermon from Windy Wendell."

I smiled back. "You're learning. It was short and to the point. Of course you will be the scandal of the county, you know."

"No doubt," he said.

On our way back, I felt relieved. Perhaps Ted Stephens is a better preacher than he gives himself credit.

We didn't get back to the farm until almost five o'clock. The afternoon ride spent with Ted Stephens had helped relieve some of my anxieties about returning to Washington. Maybe I was just growing up.

Mother was in a respectable dress with an apron and there was a delicious dinner of fried chicken waiting when we arrived. The dinner table was full of conversation and laughter. Ted Stephens and I had a special bond.

Chapter 57

Billy and Nora drove me up to the Bluemont station on New Year's Day. Mother sent Miss Eva all sorts of homemade treats. I knew Miss Eva would be delighted.

The days had flown, but I was satisfied. Christmas had been a full day with opening gifts and greeting visitors who had stopped by. Mother had not voiced any concerns about the presents I had brought and, to my surprise, had worn her showy new scarf to Stone's Chapel.

I had visited Miss Fannie, Jess and baby Daniel. They were still fixing up Miss Tizzie's place. Lockwood had changed with a new caretaker for the twins, who were doing well, and the log cabin was occupied by a new hired man and his wife. I got to see Miss Lottie and Caleb Dunn's new place on the fifty acres Mr. Lockwood had given him, and a new tenant family was in the brick house they had previously occupied. Times were changing.

My thoughts on the return to Washington were not the troubled thoughts I had when I arrived. I was eager to see Ash. I was eager to get back to work designing for the upper class women of Washington, and if Miss Eva wanted me to continue living with her in her town house, I could even do that. I was being drawn away from all that was

302

familiar with a confidence and calmness unknown to me.

Ash was waiting when the train pulled into Union Station. His beautiful smile told me he was as happy to see me as I was to see him. He carried my suitcase and took my elbow as we walked to his sporty car parked on a side street. It was New Year's Day and the city seemed quiet. After I watched him stow my case in the rumble seat, he pulled me into his arms and gave me a kiss that sent tingles from my head to my toes. "I've been waiting for you to get back, Val."

"I'm glad to be back," I said, and meant it.

He opened the door for me and then took his place in the driver's seat. Before he started the car, he looked over at me and grinned. "I've made the cutoff for spring training."

"Oh, Ash, that's wonderful," I said, and didn't mean it.

"I leave for Pompano Beach, Florida in March," he told me. "That will give us a couple of months before I have to go."

At least that is something, I thought.

It was one of those rare winter days that was sunny and mild. Instead of heading for Miss Eva's, Ash drove by the river and parked, so we could see the peaceful Potomac flow by. We stayed in the car watching the river.

Watching the river caused me to remember days gone by. I said, "Sometimes Father declared an outing and we went over to Harpers Ferry, where the Shenandoah and this same Potomac meet. I think it is one of the most beautiful spots in the country."

Ash grinned. "So did John Brown, if I remember my history."

I wasn't amused. "I don't think it was the beauty of the place that drew the heretic from Kansas."

"My weak attempt at humor," he apologized. "I've been there and I have to agree with you." He changed the subject. "Did you have a good time at home?"

I looked over at him and smiled. "It was just what I needed. I saw everyone I wanted to see. Some things have changed, but mostly it was same. I spent as much time with Ches as I could, but I know Mark is taking good care of him."

"They have stables here. You could have him transported down."

I shook my head. "He's contented where he is. That would be selfish on my part." As tempting as it sounded, I knew I would never take my beloved horse out of the hills and fields of Clarke County.

"Ash, I had a long talk with Reverend Stephens of Stone's Chapel, and he helped me sort out my quandary of staying here or going back home."

"And?" he said.

"He told me to follow the path I feel is right, so I am going to remain at Fox's Fashions and stay with Miss Eva, if she agrees."

A wide smile appeared across his attractive face. "Val, I'm glad to hear that. I want you to look at this." He pulled a velvet box from his jacket pocket. "I've been doing a lot of thinking while you've been gone." He handed me the small box and said, "Open it."

I looked at him with puzzlement on my face and hesitated before I lifted the lid. Inside was a gleaming diamond ring staring at me. "Ash, it's beautiful."

"I told you I had been doing a lot of thinking while you were away. Val, will you marry me?"

I was speechless. I stared back at the ring until I could collect myself.

"But, you're going away in a couple of months, and you will probably make the Senators. You won't be around."

"When I'm in Florida we can write letters and I can call you on Sundays. If I make the team, we'll play a lot of home games. I want to know you'll be waiting for me," he said.

"You know Nora will be getting married in the spring, and I do get concerned about Mother taking on that load. I may have to return home, whether I want to or not."

Ash put his arm around me. "Don't worry about what hasn't happened. We are here now. Let's have an engagement for a year. That will give us both time to know what direction our lives are going."

I thought about that. A year would give Mother a chance to accept the fact. That little annoying voice of 'don't get too close' went completely out of my head.

"If you don't want to accept it, I will understand," he said with a dejected tone. "Perhaps I should have given us more time."

I looked up from the box I was holding. Our faces were almost touching. "Ashton Corbin, are you out of your mind? There isn't another thing in this world that I want more than to be your girl."

These words brought a beautiful smile as he took the ring from the box and slipped it onto my finger. Sealing our troth with a warm inviting kiss, there were no more doubts.

I knew I had made the right choice.

About the author

Millie Curtis is a native of Oneida, NY and has made her home in Clarke County, Virginia since 1975.